GIRLS CAN VLOG

Lucy Locket
Online Disaster

Emma Moss loves books, cats and YouTube. In
that order – though it's a close call.

D0950996

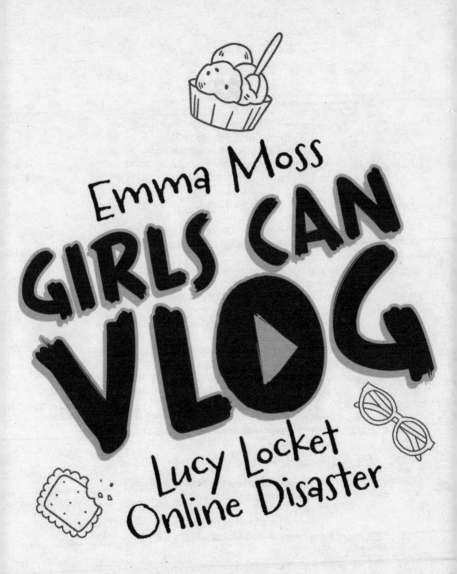

Emma Moss

GIRLS CAN VLOG

Lucy Locket
Online Disaster

MACMILLAN CHILDREN'S BOOKS

With thanks to Emily Hibbs

First published 2016 by Macmillan Children's Books
an imprint of Pan Macmillan
20 New Wharf Road, London N1 9RR
Associated companies throughout the world
www.panmacmillan.com

ISBN 978-1-5098-1491-6

Based on an original concept by Ingrid Selberg
Copyright © Ingrid Selberg Consulting Limited and Emma Young 2016

The right of Ingrid Selberg and Emma Young to be identified as the
authors of this work has been asserted by them in
accordance with the Copyright, Designs and Patents Act 1988.

Page 44 © dean bertoncelj/Shutterstock.com

3 5 7 9 8 6 4 2

A CIP catalogue record for this book is available from
the British Library.

Design by Lizzy Laczynska
Printed and bound by CPI Group (UK) Ltd, Croydon CR0 4YY

Chapter One

To: morgan_lives_here@hotmail.com

From: lucylocket@freemail.co.uk

Hey, Morgan!

How are you? I miss you SO MUCH, especially as today has been the absolute WORST day of my life. Ready – grab some jelly beans, a huge handful – because here comes a reallllly long email. Please read it carefully – you need to hear EVERY DETAIL and then give me some advice on how I am supposed to survive this year!

So, today was my first day at school since we moved back to England, and I wish it had been my last. Seriously, I WISH I WERE NEVER GOING BACK TO THAT AWFUL PLACE. You'll think I'm exaggerating, but I'm totally not. Let me talk you through the nightmare, step by step. Ready? OK, so Mom dropped me off at school and I felt super nervous. We have to wear these really gross uniforms: a weird gold blouse (can you imagine? Gold!), navy blue skirt and blazer, and worst of all these clumpy black lace-up shoes. All of which really helped my nerves – not. How can you wear your confidence on your sleeve when your sleeve is made of scratchy navy polyester? Ew!

In the school office I met a girl from my class called Hermione, who is supposed to be my 'guardian angel'. It's her job to show me around and help settle me in. She's pretty nice, though very quiet. Chinese with this amazingly shiny black hair and super-straight bangs (fringe here!). And, yes, she LOVES Harry Potter. Like, A LOT. The school looks like a museum – dark staircases and corridors, old wooden desks and furniture, grotty bathrooms (oops! Loos or toilets over here), no water fountains or vending machines. I'm telling you, it's like something out of Downton Abbey.

We have a really nice English and form teacher called Miss Piercy. You would love her: she's young and kind of ditzy – she was wearing bright yellow tights (I'm talking fluorescent). The bad news from her was that we are going to have to do a lot of public speaking – e.g. book reports and debating. The idea of this makes me feel sick to my stomach, and you know why that is! At break-time Hermione gave me the rundown on the others in our class, including some girl named Dakota, who is apparently the queen bee in our year, and Dakota's friends. Dakota is annoyingly gorgeous – she looks a bit like Kate Middleton with long, swoopy brunette hair to die for.

SO WHY IS THIS THE WORST DAY OF YOUR LIFE? you are asking. *It doesn't sound so bad.*

Just wait for it, my Yankee friend! After lunch Hermione had gone to get something from her locker and I was desperate to use the bathroom so I rushed right at the door without really checking and a BOY walked out.

'Just where do you think you're going?' he sneered at me.

'I-I-I . . .' I stammered, and dashed into the Girls' room instead.

Awkward! When I finally came out, the bell had rung and I had to race to get to my next class. I was half jogging, half looking at the map Hermione had drawn for me when suddenly I tripped on a bucket and mop standing in the corridor, slipped in the water and fell – *KERSPLATT!* – right on my butt – or bum as they call it over here. It was just outside the classroom and everyone stared at me. I wanted to melt into the floor but eventually I got up and hobbled into class . . . with a big wet patch on the back of my skirt. Morgan, we're talking ENORMOUS. And enormously DAMP.

'Look! She's wet herself!' cackled the Dakota girl. 'New girl makes a splash!' and everyone laughed.

This made me SUPER angry and without thinking I opened my mouth to yell, 'I fell and it really hurt, actually, but thanks for the sympathy.' Instead – three guesses what happens next? Yep . . . my little problem kicked in, worse than I've had it in ages.

'I fell and it r-r-r-r-r-r, rr-r-r-r-r-r,' I stammered. I took a breath and tried again. 'It r-r-r-r-r-r-r-r. R-r-r-r-r-r –' I couldn't get the word out, and at that point I gave up.

There was a shocked silence and I just stood there going bright red. Everyone was staring at me, and Dakota even had her phone out, probably texting everyone who hadn't seen it with their own eyes. I don't know which was worse, the major stammering incident or the epic dampness. Either way, I will never live this down! Hermione tried to make me feel better by saying the stain had dried out and you could hardly notice it. But I could tell that even she was shocked by how bad my stammer had gotten and basically I gave up trying to talk to anyone for the rest of the day.

Now I'm hiding in my room feeling sorry for myself – told Dad I had lots of homework but I think he knows something is wrong.

Loads of love from your miserable, embarrassed bestie,

Lucy XoX

Lucy pressed 'send' and stared blankly at the screen for a couple of minutes. She wanted Morgan to reply immediately and say something to make her feel better, but because of the time difference between England and America she knew that was unlikely.

'Lucy! Dinner!' called her mum from downstairs.

Lucy sighed, shut down her computer and gave her fluffy blue-grey cat, Foghorn, a despondent pat on the head. Just then her phone buzzed on her bedside table. Yes! A message from Morgan!

Morgan: Wait. You had to wear a GOLD shirt????????

Lucy giggled – Morgan was probably messaging her from under her desk at school – and tapped out a reply.

Lucy: UNFORTUNATELY YES.

Morgan: No wonder you're stressed 😵

Lucy: Lol

Morgan: Sorry bout your terrible day.

Lucy: Thanks, M

Morgan: Hey, do u know what would make u feel SO much better?

Lucy: Um, eating a hundred Krispy Kremes? 🙂

Morgan: Sure . . . until you puked! You know what else?

Lucy: I know what you're thinking . . . and I disagree!

'Dinner! Is Now. Served!'

Lucy: Mom calling me 4 dinner.
Gotta go but spk in abit if u can?

Morgan: Sure! We can continue
to talk about u know what ☺

Lucy rolled her eyes with a smile at the last message –
she knew what her friend was thinking and it WAS NOT
going to happen – then chucked her phone on her bed
and trudged down the stairs and into the kitchen.

'There she is! I hardly saw you after school,' said her
dad. 'You just zoomed up straight to your room.'

'Was everything OK today, sweetie?' asked Lucy's
mum gently. 'I had such a busy day at work, but I was

thinking about you the whole time.'

'Like I told Dad, it w-was . . . it was fine,' Lucy said, pouring herself a glass of squash and avoiding her mum's eye. Her good mood was evaporating fast. 'Hey, Maggie, want some juice?' she said, trying to change the conversation. Her little sister nodded eagerly and banged her plastic *Frozen* cup on the table.

'Well, we look forward to hearing about everything,' said her mum, her concerned voice starting to get on Lucy's nerves. 'I'm not saying you *did* have a bad day but if, you know, it wasn't great, don't worry – we've all been there.'

'I D-D-DIDN'T HAVE A B-B-BAD DAY!' yelled Lucy, suddenly exploding. 'Why is everyone so interested in my life anyway? C-c-can we just eat this l-l-l-lasagne please?'

She caught her mum giving her dad an anxious glance, and she knew what THAT was about. Her stammer. It only got really bad when she was feeling stressed out or anxious, and, while Lucy was trying to brush the day's events under the carpet, her stammer was telling the whole family loud and clear that something awful had happened. She wished she could go back upstairs and continue messaging Morgan – at least her best friend made her laugh.

Her dad seemed to understand that she didn't want to talk, and helpfully started a monologue about which *Toy Story* film was the best one, and as soon as Lucy could escape she raced back upstairs.

Lucy: I'm back!

Morgan: Hey girl, just in the lunch room having those curly fries you luv

Lucy: DO NOT TEASE, M. I don't think they have curly fries here 😞

Morgan: How was dinner?

Lucy: Still in bad mood and Mom making it worse

Morgan: That sucks. You need cheering up . . . time for u know what!

Lucy: Ha ha. Not happening!

Morgan: Go on . . . Make a vlog, put it online and I can watch with the rest of the gang 😃

Lucy: TOO SHY

Morgan: You could at least try . . . COME ON, LUCE 🙂

Lucy: Sorry, just not in the mood 🙁

Morgan: You were great that time you guested on my vlog

Lucy: I didn't exactly do much, M! We were just fooling around making pancakes, remember?

Morgan: U were a natural!

Lucy: You make amazing vlogs, M, but I'd be awful on my own 🙁

Morgan: TOTALLY DISAGREE. Anyway I gotta go . . . Speak soon?

Lucy: Yeah. Wish me luck for tmrw 😵

Morgan: SENDING EXTRA-CURLY CURLY FRIES OF LUCK XOX

Lucy sat cross-legged on her bed, staring into space. She felt tired and a bit annoyed – Morgan was such a great friend, but why did she think that making a stupid vlog would fix everything? Lucy had already embarrassed herself enough for one day!

No, she decided, the only way she would survive the term at Downton Abbey would be to keep her head down, walk slowly to prevent herself from slipping in giant puddles and avoid speaking completely. Foghorn stepped into her lap and gave her a pitying look. He was right – her plan wasn't exactly a recipe for fun and popularity – but it was safe and, Lucy figured, it was her only option. She went to brush her teeth, walking past the unused digital camera Morgan had given her as a goodbye present. She patted it fondly. She missed her crazy friend! But vlogging wasn't going to help her get through school again tomorrow. Mission Invisible commenced here.

Chapter Two

'W-w-wow, have a good gawp, why d-don't you,' muttered Lucy to herself the next morning. She was heading towards her classroom for registration, and avoiding the stare of a group of boys hanging out by their lockers. As they continued to gape, she realized that they hadn't even been in her class the day before – so they couldn't be mocking her about *The Incident*.

Maybe she just had something on her face? Was there a bogey hanging out of her nose? Toilet paper on her shoe? She casually patted down her hair for rogue cornflakes – at breakfast Maggie had apparently been in training for the World Cereal Spoon-flicking

Championships. But there was no errant cereal to be found. An older girl with kohl-rimmed eyes raised her eyebrows knowingly at Lucy as she passed by.

What? Lucy shrugged, mystified. *What are you all staring at?*

A loud squawk from Dakota and her friends the second she entered the classroom, followed by bursts of giggling and whispers of, 'Shhhh, she'll hear you!' from other pupils, confirmed that there was definitely something going on. Lucy fought the urge to turn round and head straight back into the hallway. Spotting Hermione with relief, she rushed up to her.

'W-w-what is it?' she whispered. 'Is it something on my f-f-face?'

'No,' said Hermione, looking up from methodically arranging the contents of her Harry Potter pencil case. 'You're fine. Have a seat.'

Lucy sat down but kept glancing around nervously. 'W-w-why were they all giggling then? P-p-people have been staring outside too.'

'Well, I don't know about them, but I can tell you that half the time I don't have a clue what Dakota and her minions are on about. They are a mystery unto themselves, have been since primary school. Kayleigh over there –' Hermione nodded to a tough-looking girl with super-straight hair and layers of concealer swathed over her bumpy skin – 'she'll pick a fight with anyone over anything, and Ameeka –' she gestured to a tall girl who somehow managed to look intensely moody even while she was giggling at Dakota's remarks – 'well . . . I've no idea really. She's the biggest mystery of all.' Hermione replaced the cap on her scented orange biro and glanced at Lucy again. 'Seriously, though, you look fine.'

But the giggles and coy glances continued even as Miss Piercy – in lime green tights today – came in and took the register. It wasn't just Dakota's friends – everyone apart from Hermione and the teacher seemed obsessed with looking in her direction. Taking her phone out, Lucy fired off a quick message to Morgan.

The whispers continued at a more subdued level through the morning lessons of English and Science. A flustered Lucy tried to keep her head down and ward off the attention, her brain racing. She didn't hear a single word any of her teachers said and instead fantasised about getting home and shutting herself in her bedroom. If Morgan were here she would figure out what was going on immediately – nice though Hermione was, she didn't seem exactly tapped in to what the other kids were up to. Lucy got the sense that most of the time she was kind of in a dream world, probably full of wizards and owls and house elves. Lucy found herself wondering if Hermione had even had any friends before she'd arrived.

But over lunch she felt grateful to have Hermione by her side, and soon the girls were absorbed in a passionate argument about whether it was Fred or

George Weasley who lost an ear in *The*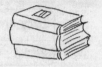
Deathly Hallows.

'Oh wait, I know how to settle this,' said Hermione. 'There's this amazing fansite where someone has compiled SO much information about the whole series, like hundreds of pages of facts. Obviously I know most of them already, but sometimes I need to double-check the odd thing like the name of Ginny's Pygmy Puff when I don't have the books with me.' She pulled her phone out of her bag and started tapping away. 'Here we go . . . oh wait, what's this? Someone's posted a YouTube link on my Facebook page – random.'

Lucy waited as Hermione stared at her screen, played the noisy video clip for a few seconds, then shoved her phone in her bag. There was a pause. 'This macaroni cheese is pretty decent for school dinners, don't you think?' Hermione said in a weirdly loud voice, taking a huge mouthful.

'Er, H-Hermione?' said Lucy. 'What did the website say? Was it Fred or George?'

'Ohyeahl'llchecklatersorryl'mstarving.'

Lucy stared at her. 'W-what was that video on your phone?'

'Nothing,' said Hermione. 'Nothing at all.'

'Well it must be s-something,' said Lucy with an anxious smile. 'You're acting k-kind of strange.'

Hermione energetically heaped salt and pepper on to her plate. Finally she mumbled, 'You don't want to know.'

The soggy school dinner felt like a lump of lead in Lucy's stomach. This was obviously bad – but what on earth was it? 'Sh-show me,' she begged. 'Please.'

Hermione sighed. 'I guess you're going to find out anyway.' She slowly delved into her bag and retrieved the phone. Loading Facebook, she handed the phone to Lucy and immediately went back to hoovering up her food.

Lucy gasped when she saw what was frozen on the screen. It was her – mousy brown hair, red face, revolting new uniform . . . and a sopping wet skirt.

Yesterday! Someone had been filming her! This couldn't be happening. She played the video from the beginning. It was all there, ten times more embarrassing than she'd remembered, her stammer seeming to go on for hours as the whole class gawped at her.

'*I fell and it r-r-r-r-r-r, rr-r-r-r-r-r . . . It r-r-r-r-r-r-r-rr–*' Her face burned as she relived the awful moment. DAKOTA! That's who had filmed this. She'd had her phone out, Lucy remembered. And now it was on YouTube, for EVERYONE to see. Her eyes filled with angry tears. 'Th-that's why everyone's been staring at m-m-me, isn't it?'

Hermione gulped. 'Maybe. I s'pose.'

'It's had s-seventy-three views on Y-youTube already. And, *oh my god*, look, s-someone's remixed it and added dance m-music!' She clutched her face in horror.

'Dakota must have sent everyone the link,' said Hermione, gently taking the phone back. 'She's always doing stuff like this. This is really low, though.'

Lucy felt sick, an odd combination of anger and panic overwhelming her. 'This is the w-worst possible way for people to get to know me. I c-can't believe she's done this – she hasn't even met me!'

'She's just a complete cow,' said Hermione with a shrug. 'She thrives off embarrassing other people. But you'll be fine – people will get to know the real you. This stupid video is deceptive and everyone will forget about it in five minutes.'

Lucy thought of Morgan. 'It's kind of f-funny, actually,' she said. 'My best friend back home, Morgan, she loves making YouTube videos – nice ones, though, just about her own life. Vlogs. And she's been encouraging me to m-make some of my own. Guess I don't need to now, though – D-D-Dakota's already done it for me! Wow, I just wish I could g-get my own back.'

'What did Morgan want you to vlog about?' asked Hermione.

'Dunno. Just s-stuff in my life, my hobbies, what I do every day,' said Lucy. She kicked the table in frustration. 'But I'd be a d-disaster online – as Dakota has just proved. To the *entire world*.'

'Sorry, but I *completely* disagree!' piped up a voice from a neighbouring table, causing Lucy to jump a mile. 'I think you'd be great!' A pretty blonde girl with a high ponytail rushed round to their table and sat down, facing Lucy. Lucy vaguely recognized her from her form group. 'Vlogging is amazing – you would love it! Do you know RedVelvet?'

Lucy nodded. 'Sure. She's g-great.'

RedVelvet was one of the most popular YouTubers on the planet – she had been a huge inspiration to Morgan, and Lucy loved her tips about self-confidence. They'd watched hundreds of her videos together.

'I know! I mean, as of last week she's got fifteen million subscribers!' continued the girl. 'It's insane!'

'I don't think Lucy's quite ready to take her on, though, Abby,' said Hermione. 'Fifteen million is a lot to aim for!'

'But that's the point. You don't have to be RedVelvet to make a vlog; ANYONE can do it,' said the girl. 'I'm Abby, by the way,' she added, beaming at Lucy. 'I promise you,' she continued, 'my brother and his mate do it all the time. They even have their own YouTube channel. They've got a pretty stupid name – Prankingstein – and they just mess around acting like complete weirdos. But people seem to like them and they're gathering a nice little army of subscribers.'

'Cool, I'll d-definitely check them out!' said Lucy with a smile. 'My best friend in America is a vlogger and she's been trying to get me to have a g-go too. She gave me a digital camera to try it, but I just don't think I have the c-confidence to pull it off. And seeing that video of me has confirmed that the whole thing would be a total f-fiasco.'

'Rubbish,' said Abby, swiping a grape from Lucy's fruit salad. 'Look at it this way. With that video, Dakota was in control, but if YOU are in control of what's recorded you can make it perfect – it can be your sweet revenge.'

'She's got a point,' said Hermione, raising an eyebrow.

'And, if you've got a camera, there's nothing stopping you!' continued Abby. 'You could just record something short and sweet for starters. Everyone will be fascinated to hear what the new girl has to say – and Dakota will be furious.'

Lucy sighed. She was almost tempted.

'Come on,' said Abby, swiping another grape, tossing it high and catching it in her mouth. 'Where do you live? I can come round after school and help you set up. Hermione will come too, won't you, Hermione?'

Hermione shrugged, and Lucy laughed. Like Morgan, Abby was not taking no for an answer. And anyway, at this point, what was the worst that could happen?

NEWSFLASH . . . VLOGGING IS GO! she messaged Morgan after lunch. Even if this was the most terrible idea in the whole of Really Terrible Ideas World, at the very least her message would make her best friend's day.

VLOG 1

Nice to meet you!

5:30

FADE IN: LUCY'S BEDROOM – NIGHT

LUCY sits on the end of her bed talking into her camera, wearing jeans and a hoodie. A sleeping FOGHORN snores in the back of shot, curled up on her pillow.

LUCY

Is this thing on? Hang on.

(*walks up to the vlogging camera and fiddles with something*)

OK, h-hopefully that's better. I haven't used this camera before. And . . . here we go.

(*clears her throat and waves*)

H-h-hi, guys! My name is Lucy – this is my room. I don't really know who I'm talking to, so it feels kind of weird – but hey! Welcome! I'm doing this video as a way to say h-h-h–

(*takes deep breath*)

HELLO.

(*rolls her eyes*)

Erm, s-s-so.

(*takes deep breath*)

Yeah, about that. I've got a s-s– a stammer. Which you probably already know about if you saw that totally emba-embarrassing video of me, which has been doing the rounds. S-someone in my class decided it would be SO hilarious to put that up on the internet (th-thanks, Dakota) – as if f-falling on my b-b-butt in front of my entire class wasn't s-s-stressful enough.

(reaches out to pat FOGHORN)

Anyway, I wanted to clear

the air and

sh-show you guys

another side of

me. My friends

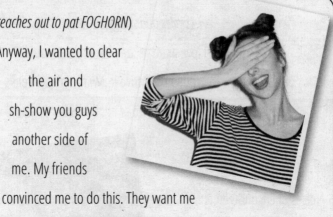

convinced me to do this. They want me

to say f-f-five interesting things about myself as that's what

some of those other famous vloggers do, like RedVelvet. She

obviously has loads of interesting th-things to talk about,

like she is the brand ambassador for a children's ch-charity.

And, secondly, she has fifteen million s-subscribers, and a

really hot boyfriend. Ha ha! Well, I guess my f-first thing is

most of the time I c-can control my stammer quite well. And

I don't go bright red like a t-tomato, and eye the door of

the room every five seconds like I d-did in school! That just

happens s-sometimes when I'm nervous. When I'm here in my

bedroom, or just chilling out with my friends, the s-s-stammers

fade away and I can get my point across more quickly. I'm just

a regular girl really.

(*smiles and shrugs*)

Second thing? I love animals, all of them! Cats, dogs, orang-utans – you n-name it, I love it. My mom's a v-vet so I guess maybe that's why. Three er . . . this is hard. Kinda blanking here.

Noises of encouragement from ABBY and HERMIONE, off camera.

LUCY (CONTINUED)

Oh, OK, so I j-j-just moved back to England from the States . . . and I'm looking forward to h-h-hanging out with some new people.

(*covers her face with her hand briefly*)

Oh my god, th-that sounded lame! What else. FOUR – I l-love singing, Taylor Swift mainly, but only ever in the shower, so you'll never hear it – ha ha! And five . . . I can touch my nose with my tongue.

(*does this and giggles*)

Anyway, I d-doubt anyone is watching, but if you are thanks for letting me being my normal self instead of the bright red flustered dork on D-D-Dakota's video! I'm going to set up a channel and upload this, p-praying I can figure out how. So I hope you like it. Oh, and this is what I look like out of my hashtag lovely u-u-uniform by the way.

FOGHORN
Meow!

FOGHORN has woken up and walks towards Lucy, meowing noisily.

LUCY
PS – that's my cat, Foghorn. Named after a f-foghorn. You can see why.

(*smiles and waves*)

Bye, everyone!

FADE OUT.

Views: 25 and counting

Subscribers: 10

Comments:

MagicMorgan: I'm so proud of you!!! More! More! More!

HashtagHermione: You go, girl! I'm putting this on Facebook.

cat_princess: AMAZING CAT! MORE VLOGS WIV THIS KITTY PLZ!!

ShyGirl1: I hate speaking in public and get tongue-tied at school too – thx for being brave and putting yourself out there!! Hope to see another vlog from you soon! xxx

(scroll down to see 8 more comments)

Chapter Three

'Lucyloo, Mommy says you have to get up now.'

Lucy groaned and turned over, burying her head under a pillow.

'Now, Lucyloo, now! Now, now, now, now, now!' sang Maggie, marching over and tugging Lucy's wrist with surprising force for a three year old.

'OK, little monster, I'll be d-down in ten minutes,' croaked Lucy. After filming her first ever YouTube video last night, she'd sent the link to Morgan and also to Hermione and Abby. She'd set up her own channel, using the name LucyLocket – a nickname her mum used to call her when she was younger, and which she already used for her email address. It was really late by the time the video uploaded and she'd crashed into bed, exhausted.

But, now that it was morning, the prospect of another day of school was making her anxious. Checking her phone in bed, she was encouraged by the number of views on her vlog – and even more so by the excited, friendly comments, especially the one from a girl admitting she hated speaking in public too. But in the cold light of day, back in the same gross uniform, would people see her as the same girl as in the video? Lucy jumped out of bed and headed for the shower. ShyGirl1 believed in her, even if she wasn't quite there yet herself!

Later, as Lucy took her seat for registration, Hermione appeared by her side, chucking her enormous school bag on the floor. Lucy noticed at least four dog-eared paperbacks fighting for space with Hermione's schoolbooks. 'So, when you texted me to say your vlog was online, I tuned in – and it was amazing!'

Lucy grinned. 'Y-you'd already seen it when we were filming!'

'I know, but it was different seeing it onscreen. When we were in your room, I thought it seemed a little – fake? – but then when I got home and watched it on my computer it looked brilliant. I watched it five times!'

'It was pretty cool,' said a boy who sat a few rows ahead, tipping his chair back to talk to them.

'Oh th-thanks. It wasn't anything special,' said Lucy, feeling a fresh wave of excitement. 'I s-still can't believe p-people have actually watched it! Mainly I just wanted to cheer m-myself up.'

'I wonder Dakota's seen it yet?' he said. 'Bet it'll wind her right up!'

As if on cue, Dakota swanned in, flicking her immaculate hair over one shoulder. She walked straight past Lucy and to her desk at the back of the room.

'Maybe she hasn't see it!' whispered Hermione, half choking on the wave of vanilla perfume Dakota had left in her wake.

'She's *definitely* seen it,' said Abby, rushing over to them. 'My mum dropped me off at the same time as hers, so I was following her through the car park and she was tapping stuff into her phone at a million miles per hour. Seriously, she nearly walked into a lamp post. I bet she's fuming that it's getting more views than hers.'

'Is it r-really?' asked Lucy. This was crazy! She didn't know what she had expectedly, exactly – definitely nothing more than a few views from her friends back home.

'Totally, I haven't checked in the last ten minutes but it was definitely in the lead last time I looked. *Told you* people would watch.'

Lucy burst out laughing at the happy, slightly boastful look on Abby's face. She couldn't have expected the vlog to do this well either, although she tried to act as if that had been the plan all along. As Miss Piercy came in and asked for quiet, Lucy just had time to fire off a quick message to Morgan.

Lucy: Loads of people are watching it!!!
What do you know, I'm a hit 😊

After the morning's lessons (during which Lucy relaxed, and even managed to answer a question without stammering – success!), she stopped off at her locker.

'H-hold this for me, will you?' she asked Hermione, shoving a textbook in her hands as she searched for her key.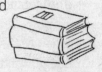

'I'll h-h-h-h-h-hold it for you, Lucy.' The unpleasant, self-satisfied voice came out of nowhere, and Lucy took a second to realize what was going on. She turned and caught sight of the supermodel-swishy hair and, seconds later, the amused smirk. Of course, Dakota was making fun of her.

'Get a life, Dakota,' snapped Hermione.

'Excuse me, was I talking to you, Harry Potter?' said Dakota, earning a scowl from Hermione. 'Get back under the stairs where you belong.'

'It's OK, H-H-Hermione,' said Lucy, her heart pounding.

'W-what do you want, Dakota?'

Dakota applied some cherry-red lipgloss, peering over Lucy's shoulder into the little mirror she'd affixed to the door of her locker. 'Just saying hello. Or should I say, h-h-h-hello! We haven't been introduced properly.' She smacked her lips contentedly and replaced the lipgloss in the hand of Kayleigh, who was hovering behind her with Ameeka. 'Of course, I DID see your little vlog. Think you're some kind of celebrity in the making, do you?'

'W-what? No!' cried Lucy.

'That's good, because RedVelvet you ain't! "Here's my overweight cat!" "I like to sing in the shower!" Please!' Dakota chuckled. 'Who cares about any of that stuff?'

'Quite a few people, actually, if the number of views Lucy's clocked up are anything to go by,' piped up Hermione, her voice trembling ever so slightly.

'Um . . . what part of GET BACK UNDER THE STAIRS do you not understand?' snapped Dakota. Kayleigh, who had been picking idly at her acne, snorted in delight.

Hermione shrank back against the locker, and Lucy jumped in to rescue her friend. 'Look, I just wanted to m-make myself f-feel better after seeing that vi-video you posted.' Her cheeks burned. 'It was r-r-r-' She stopped and took a shaky breath. 'Really horrible!'

Kayleigh did a fake sob and Ameeka rolled her eyes so dramatically she looked like she was having a fit. But a small crowd had started to gather and a few voices chimed 'Yeah – it was totally out of order!' and, 'So pathetic, Dakota,' in Lucy's defence. This was followed by a tense silence as everyone watched to see how Dakota would react.

'Well,' she said, tucking a glossy strand behind one ear, 'I'm glad that my little broadcast has set you on the road to stardom, Lucy. I'm not sure how many people will stick around for your vlogs before they get tired of having to w-w-w-w-wait for you to get the next word out, but good luck anyway, sweetie. And w-w-watch out for puddles!' She walked off, high-fiving Kayleigh and Ameeka as she went.

As the buzz of slamming locker doors picked up again, Lucy shrugged at Hermione. 'Looks like I've got off on the wrong f-foot with her, then!'

'*Can you believe that just happened?*' stage-whispered Abby, zooming over from the other end of the hall. 'She's such a drama queen!'

'Well, it's n-not like I'll be doing any more YouTube stuff, so she can find someone else to pick a fight with,' said Lucy, biting into an apple. 'I've just moved here – all I w-w-want is a quiet life!'

Abby flapped her hands so fast she nearly knocked the apple out of Lucy's hands. 'No, no, no, you have to! Do another one, I mean. RedVelvet uploads two or three videos a week! And at Christmas she does Vlogmas, which means a brand-new vlog every day in December!'

'Let's not get carried away, Abby,' muttered Hermione. Lucy could see she was still smarting from Dakota's Harry Potter jibes.

'I'm not, I promise. I just think it would be fun to see what would happen if Lucy made one more. She's got so many views on her first vlog already that she hadn't even planned properly. Imagine what would happen if she put a bit more prep into the next one.' Abby's eyes were huge with excitement.

'I – I'm n-not sure,' said Lucy. 'What would I vlog about?'

The answer came later in the day when their class was trooping back from the gym after PE. A crowd had gathered around the downstairs noticeboard. A poster read:

IT'S THE GREASE AUDITIONS!

NEXT MONDAY LUNCHTiME iN THE THEATRE. YEARS 9 AND 10. ALL ABiLiTiES WELCOME. COME ALONG AND SEE iF

YOU'RE THE ONE THAT WE WANT!

'I I-love that film,' said Lucy as a couple of boys pushed forward to put their names on the sign-up sheet.

'Let's all try out!' said Abby. 'I've been wanting to do something like this for ages, and you said you liked singing in your vlog, Lucy!'

'In the sh-sh-shower. *In private*,' said Lucy meaningfully.

'That's probably for the best,' said Dakota, appearing out of nowhere. She graciously accepted the pen from one of the boys and signed her name with an elaborate swirl. 'I've kind of got this one in the bag, so why don't you concentrate on breeding orang-utans or whatever it is that you do in your spare time, Lucy.'

'Right – that does it,' said Hermione as Dakota wafted off in her sickly vanilla cloud. She marched up and wrote down all three of their names in big confident letters. 'She'll be sorry she ever messed with "Harry Potter"!'

Lucy couldn't help but laugh at her new friend's steely determination. 'OK – what's the worst that could happen, r-right? Urgh, look. Kayleigh and Ameeka have s-signed up too. And didn't someone say that D-Dakota has private singing tuition?'

'So what?' Abby took Lucy's chin in her hand. 'Lucy. Look into my eyes. We need to focus on US, not them. And we need to practise.'

'Let go of my face!' giggled Lucy.

'I need to practise A LOT,' said Hermione, paling at the realization of what she'd just signed up for. 'I didn't even get into my school nativity play – not even as a sheep!'

'Why don't you guys c-come over again?' said Lucy. 'Tonight. We can have a sleepover-stroke-practice session, with added snacks! My parents are t-tragically thrilled that I have some new friends, so I'm sure they'll be fine with you staying over.'

'YES!' said Abby with a fist pump. 'And we can vlog the whole thing!'

VLOG 2

Sleepover Singalong!

8:33

FADE IN: LUCY'S LIVING ROOM – DAY

After school LUCY and ABBY are chatting on the sofa in jeans and cute tops, surrounded by bowls of jelly beans and Doritos. MAGGIE is zooming around, excited by all the attention.

LUCY

Hi, guys! Watch out – L-Lucy Locket is back with her SECOND VLOG. This time I'm joined by my friends Abby . . .

ABBY waves.

LUCY (CONTINUED)
and Hermione, who is helpfully filming us right now!

HERMIONE turns the camera on herself and waves before quickly turning it back.

LUCY (CONTINUED)
We're just chilling out after school, having a sleepover and –

MAGGIE darts into shot, jumps on Lucy's lap and starts chanting.

MAGGIE

Frozen! Frozen!

LUCY

We're d-dealing with my little sister who apparently wants to

talk about *Frozen*! As you can see, she is wearing her f-favourite

Princess Elsa dress, which

comes out, on average,

seventeen times a day.

Give us a twirl,

Princess Elsa.

Excitedly, MAGGIE jumps up
and down, pulling out the skirts
of her dress. The girls giggle.

ABBY

She's adorable!

LUCY

Yeah, so we're babysitting as my p-parents are out on date night! K-kind of embarrassing that they're still so romantic with each other. Anyway, guys, I wanted to say thank you for your s-supportive comments on my last vlog, which really inspired me to make another one.

ABBY rushes up to the camera so her face fills the whole screen.

ABBY

Isn't she a hashtag natural, guys? Make sure you keep sending her the love.

LUCY

Now, in today's vlog, we have a treat for you—

MAGGIE, who is now holding a struggling FOGHORN, walks into shot still chanting.

MAGGIE

FRO-ZEN – FRO-ZEN.

We can hear HERMIONE giggle as she's filming.

LUCY

Yes, Mags! *Fro-zen!*

(*pauses*)

Oh dear, this is all going a bit w-wrong. Mags, do you want to get another c-cookie from the kitchen? You can have one more.

MAGGIE zooms off, nodding crazily.

LUCY (CONTINUED)

SO, as I was saying, the three of us are auditioning for the *Grease* m-musical at school . . . and . . . I c-c-can't believe I'm saying this, but . . .

ABBY

We're going to sing a song for you guys!

LUCY

We haven't actually decided what to sing y-yet, but we've got a
few things lined up on iTunes.

MAGGIE marches back in holding an enormous cookie and a *Frozen*
DVD.

MAGGIE

Fro-zen! Fro-zen!

LUCY

(*giving MAGGIE a*

cuddle)

Not now, Mags, we've got some s-singing to practise.

(*to ABBY*)

She must have watched that DVD three hundred times by now!

MAGGIE looks on the brink of tears, her face going dark pink.

ABBY

Hmm – maybe we can play it for just a few minutes? In the background?

HERMIONE

(*from behind the camera*)

Guys, it is a SINGALONG DVD . . .

ABBY

(*her face lighting up*)

Are you thinking what I'm thinking . . . ?

LUCY has a slightly alarmed look on her face.

CUT TO: LUCY and ABBY have joined MAGGIE in makeshift *Frozen* outfits. MAGGIE has covered the girls in princess stickers and tiara headbands. The *Frozen* DVD is paused halfway, and a suspicious FOGHORN is looking on from the sofa.

LUCY

(*a bit breathless*)

Hi again, everyone! So th- thanks to my sister here . . . we've been singing some songs from *Frozen*. Not quite what we had planned, but, hey, it's still p-practice, right?

ABBY

We are sounding AMAZING. And how cool do we look?

HERMIONE

(*groaning*)

I'm so glad I'm behind the camera.

LUCY

We've saved the best one for last to sh-share with you guys.

Maggie?

MAGGIE hands LUCY the remote control, and she presses 'play'. Seconds later, the DVD launches into 'Let It Go'. Delightedly, MAGGIE breaks into song, the other two girls giggling and taking turns to sing along with her, LUCY gaining confidence as she goes. At the chorus, ABBY leaps on to the sofa, where she stands and flings her arms out. A terrified FOGHORN flees from his cushion. They all collapse with laughter.

LUCY (CONTINUED)

Ta-dah! Hope you enjoyed that more than F-Foghorn did . . .

Let us know what you think about our p-performance in the comments down below!

FADE OUT.

Views: 153 and counting

Subscribers: 45

Comments:

queen_dakota: Definitely not worried about the *Grease* auditions now. #lame

StephSaysHi: You guys are the funniest ☺

MagicMorgan: I love *Frozen* too, Maggie!

ShyGirl1: 👍 Can't wait for the next one!

(scroll down to see 10 more comments)

Chapter Four

Lucy woke up, the words of 'Let It Go' still buzzing in her head, and looked around at the slug-like forms of Abby and Hermione zonked out on the living-room floor in their sleeping bags. She grinned at the sight of them – Abby was still wearing her Princess Elsa tiara, tangled in her blonde hair, and snoring in a distinctly unprincess-like manner, while Hermione had fallen asleep with one hand in the popcorn bowl.

Quietly getting out of her own sleeping bag, she tiptoed over them and into the kitchen, where her dad was brewing some coffee and Maggie was reading a picture book to Foghorn, who seemed to be listening patiently.

'Morning, pumpkin,' Lucy's dad said as Lucy helped herself to a croissant. 'Bit of a late one, then!'

'Mmm-hmm,' she said with a guilty smile. Her parents had come home at eleven, at which point she and her friends had finally put a lid on the singing, but she knew their shrieks of laughter had gone on until the small hours as they'd excitedly uploaded the vlog and started reading the comments. 'It's so nice h-having them here, you know. We kinda wanted to make the most of it.'

Her dad handed her a plate. 'Well, your mother and I are delighted that you're making friends. We were starting to worry that nobody would ever replace Morgan.'

'D-Dad, they're not replacing Morgan!' Lucy insisted. 'In fact, th-they spoke to her on S-Skype last night. She's helping us with our vlogging.'

Mr Lockwood glanced at his daughter across the breakfast counter, slightly perplexed. 'What's it all about, then, this blogging?'

'*Vlogging*, Dad! You remember Morgan telling you back home – it's a kind of d-diary but in video format, rather than written in a journal. Yesterday we just f-filmed ourselves messing around singing and making popcorn.'

'Well, if it makes you happy . . . ' He poured himself a cup of coffee. 'And as long as you're being sensible about it. Remember, never put anything online that could show people where we live.'

'I know, Dad – it's all totally anonymous apart from our first names, don't worry.'

'Hey there, Mr Lockwood!' said Abby, entering the room. 'Hey, Maggie!'

'MFGhhhh . . . Can I have some of that coffee?' said a distinctly less awake Hermione, behind her.

The girls were followed by Lucy's mum, who also joined in the clamour for coffee. 'What are you up to today, girls?' she asked, once they were all seated and tucking into some pastries. Maggie plumped herself on to Hermione's lap.

'I'm off to the shops,' said Abby. 'I'm in urgent need of some new tops and a new eye palette, and my parents FINALLY gave me some cash to get them. I was totally running out of weekend wardrobe options.'

Lucy's mum raised an amused eyebrow at her husband.

'Can I have tops, Mommy?' said Maggie, beaming hopefully.

'No, you little fiend, you cannot!' said her mum, scooping her up and tickling her till she squealed with laughter.

'I might join you, Abby,' said Hermione. 'I need to get to a bookshop and buy something new to read that will remove all traces of *Frozen* from my mind. Forever.'

Lucy giggled as Maggie launched into 'Let it Gooooooo' at the mention of her favourite film, flinging her arms out triumphantly.

'You loved it r-really, Hermione! Maybe I'll come too – I could do with some new outfits, couldn't I, Mom?'

'But, sweetheart, you have plans today, don't you

remember?' said Mrs Lockwood.

'What? Oh – the farm thing?'

'Precisely. And you'll need to get a wriggle on – Dad will need to drive you soon.'

Lucy fiddled with her pastry. 'But, Mom, c-couldn't I start next week? Now that Hermione and Abs are here? It would be so much f-fun to go shopping all together!'

'Totally,' nodded Abby, her green eyes flashing with excitement, 'and we could go for burgers and milkshakes, and—'

She broke off, catching a stern look from Mrs Lockwood. 'Sorry, I mean, er, Lucy, you should probably do what your mum said. Sounds like fun – a farm did you say? Who doesn't love a farm?'

Mr Lockwood coughed suddenly, failing to cover up a snort of laughter.

'Springdale City Farm – it's where I work,' said Lucy's mum.

'Oh yeah, Lucy said you were a vet. That's so cool. I

bet you're really clever.' Abby's face lit up in admiration.

'The farm needs volunteers at the weekend,' explained Lucy. 'Basically f-feeding the animals and shovelling horse poo.'

Maggie giggled in delight and started shouting, 'POO, POO, POO, POO!' until Hermione managed to distract her by offering to braid her hair.

'Well, a promise is a promise, Lucy. And you love animals! I bet you enjoy it more than you think, all that fresh air and the knowledge that you're doing something good in the world,' said her father.

'Oh my god, why are you so corny, Dad? OK, fine, I'll go, but I d-don't see why you and Mom are trying to ruin my fun when I've F-FINALLY started making friends here,' Lucy said sulkily.

'Well, maybe the girls would like to join you?' said her mum. 'I'm sure they would be very welcome.'

Abby and Hermione exchanged glances. 'That's OK, we'll see Lucy at school on Monday,' gabbled Abby. 'My situation with those tops – it really is life and death.'

'Same with the books,' mumbled Hermione with a guilty smile.

'But, Luce – maybe you could get some vlog ideas while you're at the farm.' Abby checked her phone. 'So many views from last night, guys!'

'I'm not sure what people would think about me f-frolicking around in manure – I don't think I've ever seen RedVelvet do that,' said Lucy ruefully.

Lucy: Morgan – you there??

Morgan: Yes! Hi! Your *Frozen* vlog was AMAZING!

Lucy: Ha hah – thx! So, just seen the HOTTEST guy . . .

Morgan: What? Where are you?!!

Lucy: At farm where Mom works now.

Morgan: He's a farmer???

Lucy: Lol – noooo! Just helps here like me.

Morgan: Phew, thought you meant like an old man with a piece of straw in his mouth.

Lucy: Lol – as if!

Morgan: DESCRIBE HOTTIE. NAME. AGE.

Lucy: Sam. I wanna say 15ish? Blue eyes 😍

Morgan: Woo! You talk 2 him?

Lucy: Not rly – just said hi.

Morgan: Keep me posted!!!! Take a pic!!!!!

VLOG 3

FADE IN: LUCY'S BEDROOM – DAY

LUCY is on her bed, waving, her hair in a fishtail plait and wearing a blue-and-white striped top, and a red anchor-shaped pendant necklace.

LUCY

Hey, guys! So I'm back again – hope you enjoyed our *Frozen* s-singalong. Sorry my room is such a mess right now – don't have Abs here with me today to make it look perfect. I have been s-super busy, though, and that's what I wanted to v-vlog about. Today was my first day volunteering at Springdale City Farm. My mom has started working there as a vet and I'm helping out on S-S-Saturdays. It's an amazing place – a small city farm with loads of cute animals, a rescue centre for wild animals. Everybody was really friendly and helped me s-settle in. My job was to chop up veggies for the animals' lunch and also mucking out the sheds and yard. Yuck! Kind of smelly, b-but you get used to it!

And the best bit was . . . drumroll . . . a really cool s-surprise which I'm going to show you now!

LUCY slides a cardboard box into shot and rests it on her lap, opening the lid and gently lifting out a tiny creature.

LUCY (CONTINUED)

This is an orphaned baby hedgehog. They're called hoglets –
isn't that the c-cutest word ever? – and we had to bring him
home from the centre. He needs to be fed every three to four
hours with a s-syringe and my mom asked me to help.

LUCY puts on some gloves and lifts the hoglet out.

LUCY (CONTINUED)

I have to wear these s-surgical gloves when I'm handling
him – kind of ruins my outfit, oh well!
Can you see him properly?

LUCY lifts the tiny pink hoglet up to the camera.

LUCY (CONTINUED)

Isn't he cute? Say hi to everyone, little guy! Well, we're not
s-sure if it's a he or a she yet . . . but let's say it's a he, as
nobody deserves to be called it! He's only a couple of weeks
old and he only weighs a hundred grams. So tiny! He n-needs

to reach about six hundred grams to be able to survive the winter so there's a long way to go. He's sleeping in this old woolly cap next to a hot-water bottle to keep him c-cosy and warm.

LUCY puts the hedgehog back in the open box, just as FOGHORN jumps on the bed.

LUCY (CONTINUED)
H-hey, Foghorn, careful! You might scare him to death! Cats aren't dangerous to hedgehogs but Foghorn is obviously curious . . . He's p-probably a bit jealous too!

Mom says they get loads of hedgehogs at the r-rescue centre. Some of them are injured by cars or dogs, but others get their feet t-tangled in netting or get their heads stuck in plastic bottles or cups. It's really horrible and b-basically they die, unless they can get free. So d-don't chuck your trash around, because it could be a killer! And now I want your help with this little guy. We need to give him a name, so please p-put your suggestions – the crazier the better – in the comments down below and I'll let you know the winning choice next time. Gotta go now and practise for our *Grease* t-tryouts tomorrow – eek! See ya!

FADE OUT.

Views: 223 and counting

Subscribers: 107

Comments:

Amazing_Abby_xxx: Lots of views i see – that's what happenz when u feature a cute hedgehog. So glad you vlogged again ❤ ❤ ❤

MagicMorgan: Meet any OTHER cuties at the farm, Lucy ☺ ☺

lucylocket: Shut up, M!!

HashtagHermione: Can he be called Sonic?

animallover101: I vote for Spike!

animallover101: Btw I've linked this video to my cute animals channel – hope you don't mind!

lucylocket: Cool! Don't mind at all!

HashtagHermione: Or William Spike-speare? LOL

funnyinternetperson54: Barbed Wire??

funnyinternetperson54: #haha

(scroll down to see 17 more comments)

Chapter Five

'Guys, you're going to be great,' said Abby as the girls walked towards the *Grease* auditions, which were being held in the school theatre. Lucy noticed that she'd done her hair in a vintage fifties style with a little quiff. 'It's all about projecting confidence. Repeat after me. I AM A TALENTED AND SUCCESSFUL PERFORMER. Go on. I AM A TALENTED AND SUCCESSFUL PERFORMER.'

'I AM . . . um . . . never mind,' said Lucy with a giggle as a group of boys from the year above walked past. 'But th-thanks.'

'The thing is, I have no confidence to project,' said Hermione flatly.

'Yeah, I'm p-pretty nervous too,' agreed Lucy. 'Usually my s-stutter goes away when I s-sing, but what if it doesn't today?'

Abby put an arm round each girl. 'Guys! Just have fun like on our sleepover vlog. You don't have to be the world's best singer – you just need to prove you have stage presence.'

She's like a judge from a reality TV show, thought Lucy fondly.

'You're so right, Abby,' trilled Dakota as she walked past them, flanked by Kayleigh and Ameeka. 'I mean obviously, as my singing teacher says, *I* have a natural gift, but there are loads of parts and unfortunately the director will be forced to cast some very average people.' She looked at Hermione. 'Or, worse yet, sub-average.'

'Yeah, D, your light will shine, like, four hundred times brighter compared to these losers,' said Kayleigh as Dakota pushed her way through to the front of the queue.

'Five hundred times, even,' purred Ameeka, following behind them.

Abby rolled her eyes. 'Are they for real? Honestly!'

As they entered the theatre and were ushered up on stage, Lucy suddenly felt a wave of nerves overcome her. *WhatamIdoingwhatamIdoingwhatamIdoing?* she thought, fighting a very acute urge to run for the door. But noticing that Hermione looked even more panicked, she gave her a reassuring smile and remembered they were all in this together.

Dressed in a slinky wrap dress, Ms Kusama, the school's new head of drama, smiled at the group of pupils assembled before her. 'It's wonderful to see so many of you here – especially as we are looking to up our game with the Years Nine and Ten school production,' she trilled. 'Last year's performance of *Mamma Mia* left, shall we say, something to be desired . . . but as of today we're going to act like consummate professionals!' Lucy caught Hermione's eye and stifled a slightly hysterical giggle. 'Now, today

I'd like to start by offering you a choice of two songs from *Grease* – 'Look at Me, I'm Sandra Dee' and 'Greased Lightnin'' – I'm sure you'll be familiar with the words, but here are some lyric sheets just in case. I'll see you one by one and then you are free to go – we'll post the results later. Please form an orderly queue . . . OK, Dakota – looks like you're up first. Good luck, everyone!'

The audition had been all right, Lucy reflected in PE, as she stood on the rounders field keeping a lazy eye on the game. Not too scary, and she had managed not to stammer by concentrating hard on her singing. It had been quite funny actually watching some of the boys . . . all trying to out-cool each other as potential leather-jacketed T-Birds. Suddenly an image of Sam entered her mind. Well, if she were honest, he'd entered her mind a few times – OK, a *lot* of times – since she'd seen him at the farm on Saturday. She was counting down the days until she'd see him again, even though the thought of talking to him made her stomach fall into her shoes. He would look so hot as Danny from *Grease*, in a leather jacket, with his dark hair slicked back . . . She pictured him flinging her across the dance floor, her fifties-style skirt flaring out around her, the music getting faster and faster, his cute grin getting wider by the second . . .

'Earth to Lucy!' cried Abby, running over.

'Huh – what?'

'The ball? You're meant to, you know, catch it? It practically landed on your head!'

'S-sorry – I was a million miles away,' Lucy said with an embarrassed giggle, scooping up the ball and throwing it back to the bowler. 'H-how are you feeling about your audition?'

Abby did some leg stretches. 'Pretty good I think . . . but I saw poor Hermione earlier and she said she clammed up completely. Couldn't sing a single note and just stood there panicking.'

'Aw – I don't think she even WANTS to get in!'

'Totally – she'd rather have her nose in a book than be anywhere near an audience.' A curious look crept over Abby's face. 'So, what were you daydreaming about just now when you were nearly decapitated by that ball?'

'Oh, n-nothing – just zoned out!' Lucy wasn't ready to tell Abby about Sam, and anyway there was nothing to tell and probably never would be. It felt easier to share her secret crush with Morgan who was safely overseas.

'Well, good, as I wanted to go through some vlog ideas with you.' Abby ran to get the ball, and came back breathlessly. 'I've put some photos up on Instagram to inspire us and—'

'Hey, guys!' One of the rounders players ran after Abby, interrupting her with a friendly wave. 'Abby! And, Lucy, right? I'm Jessie,' she announced, jogging up and down on the spot, her hundreds of tiny braids jumping around. 'I've been watching your vlogs and I'm a HUGE fan.' Abby and Lucy exchanged surprised glances. 'Well, I loved the *Frozen* one at least – have to say you kind of lost me with that hedgehog baby. Weird pink-looking thing. And that first one of you at school, Lucy – hashtag *awkward*! What a car crash!'

Lucy flinched. 'W-well I didn't CHOOSE for that to go online, obv-obviously.'

'I know, I'm just messing with you! Dakota is a total crazy person!' Jessie stopped jogging and started doing lunges – it was making Lucy tired just to look at her. The girl fizzed with energy. 'So I heard you saying you were looking for ideas . . . ' Abby shrugged guiltily in a 'Who, me?' gesture. 'Why don't you do a food challenge video next? Me and my brother watch loads of them after school – people eating gross foods and stuff! It's great – sometimes they even puke!'

'Not sure about that,' said Abby, making a face. 'But maybe you're on to something with the food angle . . . '

'H-hey I know!' said Lucy. 'What about baking? Is that a big d-deal over here like it is in the States? People there are obsessed with c-cupcakes!'

Abby grinned. 'I think that trend has reached our shores, yes – and actually Hermione loves baking, so maybe she can help us. Let's ask her later. We need to think recipes, timings, aprons . . . ' As she started to brainstorm, the rounders ball landed at her feet. ' . . . Ingredients, a cute tablecloth . . . ' The ball stayed where it was, Abby completely oblivious to the frustrated cries of her team.

Eventually Jessie picked it up for her and threw it back, then, 'This is kind of cheeky,' she said, interrupting Abby mid-flow. 'But can I be in the vlog too? As it was my idea – kind of?'

Lucy looked at Abby, who shrugged happily. 'OK, you're in!' said Lucy. 'The m-more the merrier.'

Later, after Lucy's dad had taken them shopping for ingredients, the girls started preparing for the vlog.

'Four of you now I see,' Mr Lockwood said as they were unpacking the bags. 'My daughter Lucy – Miss Popularity in action!'

Mortified, Lucy swiftly banished him to his writing den. Why did he have to keep referring to the fact that she'd made some friends as if it were some massive achievement? So embarrassing!

Lucy poured the different coloured sprinkles into little bowls. There was something else bothering her too, which had been nagging at her since breakfast. She'd overhead her mum saying the city farm was losing some funding. If they had to lose staff, or shut down completely, her job would be on the line. And if she lost her job they might have to move to a different town as there weren't many vet jobs going in this area. Lucy couldn't bear the thought of having to move again, just as she'd started making such great friends.

'Ready when you are, Lucy Locket,' shouted Abby, fastening her apron. 'Let me touch up your blusher.' And, just like that, Lucy forgot her troubles and prepared to greet her viewers.

VLOG 4

Cupcake Challenge! 11:00

FADE IN: LUCY'S KITCHEN – DAY

The kitchen is very neat with large, clean surfaces. Filming with webcam to start.

LUCY

Hi, everyone! Today you are lucky enough to have *four* of our b-beautiful faces to look at: Hermione, Jessie and Abby are also here. Say h-hi, everybody!

The girls all shout HELLO, wave at the camera and dance around like complete lunatics. JESSIE is doing star jumps.

LUCY (CONTINUED)

OK, so in a minute I'll tell you why we're in the k-kitchen today, but first I promised to let you know the winning name for the hoglet, who it turns out really is a boy. D-d-drum roll please . . . the winning name is: Barbed Wire! Thanks to funnyinternetperson54 for the awesome suggestion, and I'm p-proud to say that Barbed Wire is putting on weight every week.

So, brilliantly named hedgehogs aside, now it's time for our d-delicious challenge. Hermione – over to you!

HERMIONE walks up to the camera. She looks a bit nervous and very serious. The others are giggling in the background and putting on aprons. LUCY joins them.

HERMIONE

Uh, thanks, Lucy. Hi, Lucy's fans! Apparently everyone thinks I'm quite a good baker so when we decided to do this challenge Lucy nominated me to be the judge. I don't think I'm that good, though.

JESSIE

Yes you are – you're amazing! I remember that time you made Harry-Potter-themed cookies for the whole class.

HERMIONE

That *was* fun . . . it was really hard to get those strawberry laces into a lightning-bolt shape for Harry's scar, though! OK, so today we are doing the Great Cupcake Challenge! Just now I made the chocolate cupcakes we need for this competition.

ABBY presents the cupcakes on a tray with a dramatic flourish.

ABBY

How yummy do these look?

HERMIONE

The aim is to decorate the cupcakes using the icing, sprinkles and other decorations provided. I've already let them cool so that the icing will sit properly and not melt off the edges. Once they are decorated, the best cupcake will win!

Camera cuts to the table where the ingredients are laid out in front of the girls.

HERMIONE (CONTINUED)

So here we have – two cupcakes each – including a spare in case anyone messes up.

HERMIONE looks pointedly at JESSIE, who shrugs dramatically in a '*WHAT?*' gesture. Somehow JESSIE already has icing sugar all over her face.

HERMIONE (CONTINUED)

Then we have one icing bag each to be filled with your icing of choice. You'll need to mix in the food colouring first – we stocked up on every colour of the rainbow! Plus a selection of sprinkles, glitter and edible flowers. And the final thing about this challenge – it's timed! You guys will have three minutes to complete your designs.

Ready? Steady! Decorate!

HERMIONE picks up the camera, now in handheld mode. We see JESSIE dropping icing sugar into a bowl, half of it missing completely, adding water and most of the bottle of red food colouring. She is muttering under her breath, sweeping great swathes of spilt sugar off her jeans.

LUCY is carefully mixing her icing, trying not to laugh at JESSIE. ABBY hasn't started yet, she is too busy looking at the food colouring bottles and deciding which shade to choose.

HERMIONE (CONTINUED)
(*more confidently*)
Time is ticking, Abby! It's only a cupcake – you're not deciding
on the right shade of hair dye! Ladies and gents, she's going for
the lavender. A fine choice! Now, girls, two minutes to go: get
that icing in the bag. *GO, GO, GO!*

The girls spoon the mixtures into the icing bags, LUCY grinning as most of JESSIE's ends up on the outside of the bag. She helps her to wipe off the excess.

HERMIONE (CONTINUED)
And now – ice for your life!

The icing is piped on, neat swirls by LUCY, in little dots by ABBY, and in one big red blob which comes out in one go from JESSIE's tube. She tries again a little more successfully on her second cupcake, though the result is still the messiest by far.

HERMIONE (CONTINUED)

Well done, everybody! Now for the sprinkles – go, go, go!
Thirty seconds! Watch out, Mary Berry!

Giggling now, dodging FOGHORN who has come in and is trying to jump on the counter, the girls run around grabbing the various decorations and getting to work. They hurry to put on the finishing touches . . .

HERMIONE (CONTINUED)

And time's up! Cakes down! OK, viewers, please join me as we

have a look at all three beautiful cupcakes . . . aaaand I think

we have a winner. That practice cupcake DID come in handy . . .

Congratulations, Jessie! I'm awarding you first prize for what

looks like roadkill on a cupcake – full marks for originality.

Camera zooms in on the cupcake, which is drenched in blood-red icing
with a thumbprint of sprinkles embedded deep in the icing.

ABBY

What? But that's revolting! Look how pretty mine is!'

JESSIE is running around the kitchen cheering and punching the air. LUCY gets the camera back from HERMIONE.

LUCY

W-well, interesting choice there, Hermione. I thought mine wasn't bad either, but I guess the judge's decision is f-final. Congratulations, Jessie, and see you next time, guys! If you enjoyed this video, please g-give us a thumbs up!'

ABBY stuffs a cupcake into LUCY's mouth and they all burst out laughing.

ABBY

Vote for YOUR winner in the comments down below!

FADE OUT.

Views: 295 and counting
Subscribers: 234

Comments:

StephSaysHi: Ha ha you guys are crazy – you shd be on TV!!! Dying!

funnyinternetperson54: Yesss! What do I win?

clemthebestX: Bring the leftovers into school on Monday PLZZZZ

CookieMonster: Next time bake cookies!

pink_sprinkles: Roadkill yuck! 👎. Abby should have won! 👍 up!

billythekid: How about a pizza challenge??? 🍕 🍕 🍕

(scroll down to see 12 more comments)

Chapter Six

Lucy pulled on her favourite faded jeans with the hole in the knee, a grey T-shirt and a snug navy fleece. She was getting ready for her second volunteer day at Springdale and felt a million times more excited than last time. She'd had a great week in between – a blur of vlogging, dreaming about vlogging, talking about vlogging, reading comments, counting subscribers – and now Hot-Sam-Who-Would-Look-Fit-As-Danny-From-*Grease* Day had finally arrived. The day they might have a proper conversation! She felt a hundred butterflies taking flight in her stomach as she smoothed her hair down and practised talking into her full-length mirror.

'H-hi, S-Sam, how's your week been?' she said in such an odd, high-pitched voice that Foghorn awoke abruptly from napping on the bed and meowed in alarm.

'Hmm . . . let's try that again. What would RedVelvet do?' she muttered. She thought back to the YouTuber's 'confidence DIY' videos, which had helped her in the past. 'Take a breath, just be yourself, b-be natural . . .' She cleared her throat and looked confidently at her reflection. 'Hi, Sam! What's up!' she said breezily, then cringed. She'd never had a boyfriend before – well, if you didn't count Peter Karlowsky back in the US who'd shared his Twizzlers with her every break-time – and, while she didn't mind talking to boys, she knew that her stammer got worse when she talked to someone she liked. *And what am I meant to talk to him about, anyway?* she panicked.

But as she packed her vlogging camera into her rucksack, along with a few snacks and a bottle of water, an idea struck her. Of course! She'd been planning to shoot some footage of the animals at the farm for a new vlog – and she could interview Sam about his work there! It was the perfect excuse to talk to him – and she never felt more confident than when she was vlogging – so hopefully the sick feeling threatening to engulf her would simply disappear and her voice would hold out.

She slicked on some clear lipgloss, blew a kiss to Foghorn and rushed downstairs, where her dad was waiting to give her a lift.

Morgan: It's farmyard-flirting o'clock!! Good luck today!

Lucy: What are you still doing up??
Must be late over there.

Morgan: Supporting my overseas friend – what else?

Lucy: Aww, love you! Morgan, I am so nervous!

Lucy: Heeelp me!

> **Morgan:** Sending you a four-leaved clover . . . 🍀 xxx

> **Morgan:** Hope he's as hot as you remember . . .

He IS as hot as I remember, thought Lucy with a start as she jumped out of the car and immediately caught sight of Sam speaking with a little girl on horseback. The girl looked nervous and Sam was giving her a reassuring smile while talking her through the basics. He was tall and broad-shouldered, yet so gentle-looking. As he put his hand through his hair, it scruffed up adorably, and Lucy realized how unaware he was of his gorgeousness – she bet he never even looked in a mirror, unlike some of the posers at school. He would come across so well on her vlog!

Dragging herself away before he caught her staring like a weirdo, she went to store her rucksack in the lockers and fixed herself a cup of tea as she waited for the arrival of Bea – another volunteer who allocated the jobs on Saturdays.

'Hey, mind if I join you?'

Lucy nearly dropped her plastic cup as Sam came up beside her. 'H-hey, Sam – no, help yourself.'

There was silence as he filled his cup from one of the Thermoses put by for the volunteers, and Lucy wondered how to bring up the subject of her vlog.

'So – ready for your second day?' he asked.

'S-sure, I'm excited . . . C-c-can't wait to get s-s-started.'

There was another pause. This was the most they'd ever said to each other, and Lucy could tell that Sam was figuring out that she had a stammer. Her cheeks started getting warm. He was probably finding it really awkward and she bet he would find a reason to end the conversation, as if he were doing her a favour. Quite a few people reacted like that when she first met them.

'Your mum works here, right?'

Or maybe not! Lucy relaxed again. 'Yep, she's a vet. We j-just moved a few weeks ago s-so she could take the job.'

'Cool. I'd love to keep working with animals when I'm older.'

He didn't seem fazed at all by her stammer, and Lucy was grateful to him for not saying anything about it.

'Me too . . . m-maybe I'll end up here like my mom!' Before she knew what she was doing she asked, 'H-hey, not to put a d-downer on things . . . but do you know anything about the money pr-problems here?'

An anxious look passed over Sam's face. 'There's been a rumour . . . Why, what do you know?'

'Not much, j-just something my mom mentioned about hoping that the farm will be able to s-stay open. She'd hate to m-move jobs again – she loves it here.'

'Yeah, I bet,' said Sam sympathetically. 'It would be the worst if it had to close – there's a lot of important community outreach stuff going on here.'

This was the perfect time for Lucy to mention the vlog interview – she could tell Sam would be brilliant at talking about the farm. But as she wondered about how to phrase the question Bea bustled in, rifling through the papers on her clipboard.

'Sorry I'm late, you guys. Lucy – are you OK to muck out Pets Corner? Messy work but you get to hang out with the cute and fluffies!'

'Sure,' said Lucy, heading over to get the broom. She'd ask Sam about the interview later, she decided. But as she headed over to the tool cupboard she could hear him discussing his afternoon students with Bea. His friendly tone had changed.

'I don't want her in the class again, Bea. Last week she was texting while riding – again! This is why I prefer teaching the younger kids!'

'Lauren IS slightly addicted to her phone,' said Bea. 'Let's just make sure it's confiscated before the class today – I agree that it's a danger.'

Sam sighed. 'Really uncool. And also it's like – is horse riding not FUN enough for you? I hate the way people always assume something more interesting is happening on their phones. It's so shallow! You've got a beautiful animal to ride, it's a sunny day – just enjoy the moment.'

Bea laughed. 'You're an original, Sam, one lone boy fighting back against the tide of social media.'

'I know, I know, it's just . . . all those people texting and watching hours of YouTube instead of actually DOING THINGS need to get a life! Maybe that's harsh, but it's what I think.' Sam shrugged and disappeared off to the stables.

Seconds later, Lucy walked out to Pets Corner, her heart sinking to the bottom of her wellies. She didn't think she'd be sharing her new hobby with Sam any time soon – let alone asking him to star in her farm vlog.

VLOG 5

Visit to Springdale City Farm!
Cute Animals Alert!

10:20

FADE IN: SPRINGDALE CITY FARM – DAY

LUCY is dressed in jeans, hoodie and wellies at the entrance sign for Springdale City Farm, vlogging camera on selfie mode.

LUCY

Hi, guys! We had some f-fantastic feedback on the Cupcake Challenge we did last week. It was so much fun and I can't wait to do another one soon. If you've got any s-suggestions for the next challenge, put them in the comments box down below. I was also really excited by your likes following my v-vlog about Barbed Wire the hedgehog – so today I thought I'd take you on l-location and show you Springdale City Farm, where he was rescued, and introduce you to some of the animals and p-people who work here.

CUT TO: LUCY's point of view from handheld camera. Walking into farm.

LUCY (CONTINUED)

It's the f-first time I've tried filming outside so please b-bear with me! I'm still learning how to use this camera and I'm sorry if it's all a bit wobbly. I'm just going to show you the whole f-farm so you can see all the areas.

CUT TO: panning shot of farm from left to right.

LUCY (CONTINUED)

Over there are the riding s-stables, the outer enclosures for the larger farm animals and the l-llamas, the animal rescue centre and hospital, and the c-cafe. And first up today is a visit to the Pets Corner, which I was mucking out earlier this morning. (I *think* I've washed off all the poo from my boots! Classy person that I am!) This is home to some

c-cuddly farm animals and pets that little kids can get c-close to and even stroke. We have to make sure that the kids treat the animals gently and that no one ever feeds them any food except what we've p-prepared. Anyway, meet Snowdrop and Toffee, our two pygmy goats, who are very c-curious and cheeky; B-Belle and Bambi, our two lambs; Flopsy, Mopsy and Cottontail the lop-eared rabbits – don't you love their long droopy ears? – and, l-lastly, here are some guinea pigs – but I can't remember all their names.

CUT TO: point of view drops suddenly and is jiggled and unfocused before stabilizing.

LUCY (CONTINUED)

Help! Whoops! Th-that was a close call. Snowdrop just gave me a sneaky headbutt from behind and I nearly stacked it. I'm getting f-famous for that!

LUCY giggles.

LUCY (CONTINUED)

I want you to meet Bea, who is showing me the ropes here.

BEA waves to camera, holding a guinea pig.

LUCY (CONTINUED)

Bea, how long have you been working at Springdale?

BEA

Just over two years. I started out with the farm animals, but now I'm loving looking after the cuddlies. We all have so much fun.

LUCY

Thanks, Bea. There are lots of cool people working here at the f-farm, including some really f-fit boys, especially over at the stables.

LUCY and BEA exchange glances and giggle.

LUCY (CONTINUED)

Oops! P-probably shouldn't have said that! B-better get back to

work here mucking out this yard – it's a bit smelly so you gotta

hold your nose! See you later!

HALF-SECOND BREAK

LUCY (CONTINUED)

Hi! Back again. So now we'll h-head over to the cafe for our

lunch break. I'm starving! H-here's where we get to meet the

other volunteers. Oh no!

ZOOM TO: a small group of volunteers including a few good-looking

boys. LUCY's camera lingers on SAM.

LUCY (CONTINUED)

S-sorry about that, f-folks. I don't want anyone to feel

uncomfortable about my f-filming so am trying to keep it low-key. But that was Daisy, Nick and Sam . . . who all work here.

See you later!

The screen goes black –
LUCY has shoved the
camera in her pocket,
but she's forgotten
to turn it off, so the
following conversation
is recorded.

DAISY

So, Lucy, have you met Sam yet?

LUCY

Y-y-yes. Hi, Sam. How's your d-day going?

SAM

Good – I'm always happy when I'm around horses.

Whoa, that sounds cheesy!

DAISY

Sam's especially good at helping with the riding for disabled lessons. He has a real knack – both with horses and people.

SAM

(*sounding embarrassed*)

Oh, it's nothing special. What about you, Lucy? Do you like riding?

LUCY

I haven't done it much. But I d-do love horses.

SAM

Well, you should come over to the stables and meet ours sometime.

LUCY

S-sure, I-I – I'd love to!

FADE OUT.

Views: 197 and counting

Subscribers: 271

Comments:

StephSaysHi: Love those lop-ears! So cute!

Amazing_Abby_xxx: Fit boys indeed! no wonder you luv it there 😊

ShyGirl1: So cool that you do this with your spare time x

MagicMorgan: your first outside vlog – YAYYYYYY!!

queen_dakota: Well, if it isn't Miss Muck. Bet you smell amazing – not!

animallover101: Those pygmy goats ♥ ♥

(scroll down to see 14 more comments)

Chapter Seven

'The names are up! The names are up!' shouted Abby, zooming into the cafeteria on Monday lunchtime and grabbing Lucy and Hermione by the arm. 'I just heard – they're on the noticeboard! Come *on*!'

'Where's the fire?' said Jessie, looking on in amusement as she bit into her sandwich.

'*Grease,*' explained Hermione warily, putting down the enormous paperback in which she'd been immersed over lunch. 'We tried out and apparently it's worth dislocating our necks to see if we made it. Even though I couldn't actually sing a note in my audition so it will be some serious barrel-scraping if they give me a part.'

'Ha – rather you than me!' said Jessie. She put her legs up on the table and sat back in her chair. 'Guess I'll just eat your chips, then, as you have to leave in such a hurry. Good luck!'

'Remind me why we did this again?' groaned Hermione as they left the canteen.

Lucy threw an arm round her friend. 'Come on, Hermione – you're the one who signed us up, r-remember! Don't be so negative – you never know!'

A haze of vanilla greeted Lucy, Abby and Hermione as they arrived at the noticeboard, struggling to see over the crowd of heads. 'So I got Rizzo – she's the most important character, much more than Sandy,' Dakota was saying at the top of her voice. 'Her character has, like, so much depth and complexity.' Lucy sighed. The arrogant voice continued. 'And look, Kayleigh, you got Jan, one of the other Pink Ladies!' Kayleigh gave a whoop. As Dakota's number two this suited her perfectly. 'And OH MY GOD – Ameeka – you've got Marty, she's a Pink

Lady too! Those extra lessons we had paid off!' Ameeka just about forced a smile and the girls all hugged as Lucy rolled her eyes at Hermione.

Dakota glanced at the board again. 'Frenchy will be played by . . . this can't be right . . . Lucy Lockwood? Wait. As in, L-L-Lucy L-L-Lockwood? What a joke.'

'Disaster more like!' snorted Kayleigh.

Lucy gasped and jostled her way forward. She hadn't for a second thought that she would have been given a speaking part, much less one of the Pink Ladies! If anything, she'd imagined being one of the *Grease* students who just had to hang out in the back of the big scenes. But Dakota was right – there was her name, bold as anything.

'Amazing!' cried Hermione, her gloominess forgotten. 'I told you your singing was great. Frenchy's the one who accidentally dyes her hair pink – how cool is that!'

'They're probably including you to be politically correct,' Dakota told Lucy with a smirk. 'You know, because of your stammer, to show that the school works with people of all "abilities".'

'Yeah,' said Kayleigh with a grin. 'You can probably get a disabled parking space too.'

Ignoring them – she was going to be a Pink Lady! – Lucy looked around for Abby and spotted her standing off to the side.

'What about you, Abs?' she said, going over. 'Did you get Sandy?'

'No . . . ' said Abby, playing with a loose string on her jumper sleeve. 'That went to someone in the year above. Maxine.'

'S-s-so who are you, then?' asked Lucy, craning to look back at the list.

Abby looked uncomfortable. 'I'm just in the chorus,' she said quietly. 'Not a speaking part. It's no big deal, really.'

'What? N-no, that can't be right.'

'Well, that's what it says on the board. Hermione didn't even make the chorus.'

'That's because I'm *terrible* at singing,' said Hermione,

hearing the end of their conversation. 'I told you: I'm about as talented as Ron Weasley is at reading tea leaves. But, seriously, bad luck, Abs – I don't know what they were thinking not casting you.'

As they stood there in awkward silence, Dakota, Kayleigh and Ameeka turned from the noticeboard and walked past. Then, in what seemed to be a perfectly choreographed move, they stopped at the same moment and swivelled towards Lucy with an accusing glare.

'Lucy Lockjaw – or whatever your name is,' said Dakota, 'what you see before you –' she gestured at her group – 'represents the crème de la crème of acting at this school. Any evidence of your performance weakening our star power will not be treated lightly. See you at rehearsals – and try not to let your little s-s-s-s-speech impediment get in the way. We don't want the poor front row to be wiping your spit off their faces.'

Kayleigh laughed in delight as Ameeka mimed wiping spit off her brow. The trio moved off, leaving the other students to stare at Lucy with a mix of shock, curiosity and pity.

'Lucy, you are AMAZING,' said Hermione fiercely as the colour drained from Lucy's cheeks. 'You are going to make us all proud. Don't listen to Diva Dakota – she obviously has issues. I reckon she's disappointed not to get Sandy so she's taking it out on you.'

'Yeah. Ignore her, Luce – and, uh, well done,' said Abby, stumbling over the last bit of the sentence. 'I'm really just . . . so . . . happy for you.' She smiled weakly, not meeting Lucy's eye. 'Anyway, we'd better get going – double maths won't wait forever!'

Lucy looked after her anxiously and, as the crowds dispersed, she found herself wondering just what exactly she had got herself into. So much for keeping her head down this term!

Lucy: OMG I got into *Grease*!

Morgan: Wooooooooooooooohoo! Which part?

Lucy: Frenchy!

Morgan: Aah my fave Pink Lady! U'll be amazing ☺

Lucy: Bit awkward tho – Abs didn't get a part and she's the one who really wanted one . . . ⊗

Morgan: Poor Abby. Sure she's happy 4 u tho.

Lucy: Yeah says she is – I'm just feeling guilty. And scared of having so many lines . . .

Morgan: Treat it like a vlog and u'll be fine ☺

Lucy put down her phone as the maths teacher walked into the classroom for the first lesson of the afternoon. As he started talking animatedly about Pythagoras's theorem (*HOW can someone get so excited about a triangle?* she marvelled), she found herself switching off and thinking about Sam. Sam and his cute scruffy hair, Sam who was so good with kids . . . Sam who would probably be shocked by the numerous texts she exchanged daily with Morgan, she realized miserably, inadvertently sighing out loud. Not to mention her vlogging. She'd chosen to hide her Springdale filming from him, and it was best that he didn't find out about her YouTube channel if she really wanted a shot at impressing him. Anxiously, she twisted a piece of paper in her hands.

'What's wrong?' mouthed Hermione from the next desk over. 'You look mega-stressed!'

'Nothing!' she mouthed back. She didn't feel like opening up about Sam, and she didn't think Hermione would be the world's biggest boy expert anyway.

'Don't worry about Abby – she'll be fine!'

'It's not that!'

'What, then?'

'You wouldn't understand. D-doesn't matter!'

'You can trust me!'

'Seriously, d-don't worry about it.'

Hermione held her gaze for a second, a hurt look slowly crossing her face, before she turned her head and stared intently at the numbers on the whiteboard.

Great, thought Lucy. *She's annoyed*.

It felt as if she were upsetting all her friends today.

The day seemed to go from bad to worse. Lucy was sure Abby was avoiding her, rushing off after lessons instead of hanging around for their usual end-of-school vlogging debrief. And there was worrying news at home. Upon hearing the *Grease* announcement, her parents were predictably way too excited, and her mum insisted on cooking Lucy's favourite for dinner – fish pie.

'After the day I've had, it's great to hear some good news,' said Mrs Lockwood as they began to eat. 'Tell us some more about the part – it's been years since I saw that movie!'

'Frenchy's one of the Pink L-Ladies, Mom,' said Lucy. 'She's really funny. But . . . why did you have a b-bad day?'

Her parents exchanged glances, and her mum sighed. 'Look, it's early days and I don't want to worry you, but I've discussed it with your dad and I guess it's only fair to tell you – Springdale is at risk of closure.'

Lucy put down her fork and felt a shiver come over her. So what she'd overheard was true.

'Does that mean we might have to m-move again? So you can g-get another job?'

'No, sweetie,' said her mum, reaching out her hand. 'Well, not immediately anyway – nothing will happen for months, and I'm sure the directors of the farm will secure the necessary funding from somewhere in the meantime.'

'There has to be a solution,' added Mr Lockwood, nodding. 'And my screenplay is coming along nicely, so even if something happens to your mom's job I'm sure we'll be able to stay here. Don't worry, Pink Lady.'

'Yes, don't worry, Lucyloo,' piped up Maggie seriously.

Lucy smiled at her sister and wished everything were as easy as it seemed to be in Maggie's little make-believe world. Her dad was a talented writer, but she knew they relied on her mum's job for regular income, and as she tried to force down her fish pie she was panicking.

I don't want to move . . . but maybe it's better if we do – otherwise, will Abby ever forgive me for getting a part in Grease *instead of her? Will Dakota make my life a living hell during rehearsals? Will Sam suddenly realize how stupid and shallow I am?*

Her throat hurt and she longed for the end of her celebratory dinner so she could go to bed. She knew she needed to put up a new vlog soon – Jessie had texted to remind her that the viewers would be expecting new content by now. But tonight Lucy Locket was out of ideas, and out of energy.

VLOG 6

Under the Weather ☒ 4:15

FADE IN: LUCY'S ROOM – NIGHT

LUCY is in her fluffy pale grey dressing gown, propped up on her pillows in bed, with FOGHORN purring on top of the duvet near her head. When LUCY speaks, she sounds croaky.

LUCY

Hi, guys, as you can probably tell I'm not feeling b-brilliant today, I came down with this horrible cold yesterday and my throat is really sore. I've been d-drinking some honey and lemon, but it doesn't seem to be doing much. Luckily Foghorn is a very cute and attentive nurse. He's much quieter than usual as you can see. A purr-fect hot-water bottle! Say hi, Foghorn!

LUCY nudges
FOGHORN towards
the camera.

LUCY (CONTINUED)

Because I've been ill I haven't been up to much, and I wasn't going to vlog at all today, but I wanted to tell you the good news about Barbed Wire – he's grown to nearly 250g now. Amazing!

LUCY coughs.

LUCY (CONTINUED)

He's downstairs, but I'll show him to you again soon and you'll

barely recognize him. He's so c-cute!

LUCY breaks off into a coughing fit.

LUCY (CONTINUED)

Sorry about that! I also wanted to share the slightly s-scary

news that, amazingly, I got a part in *Grease* – so you'll be

hearing more about that soon.

LUCY looks a bit pale and starts coughing again. Her dad can be heard

shouting, 'Lucy, get some rest!'

LUCY (CONTINUED)

Er, sorry – that was my dad. I'd better go. Hope you don't

have to wait too long for my next vlog. I'm getting l-loads

of new subscribers, which I am thrilled about, so thanks

to everyone watching and it's really important to me that

there is enough new stuff on my ch-channel for you

guys to want to keep tuning in. Bye for now!

LUCY waves FOGHORN's paw at the screen, still coughing.

FADE OUT.

Views: 109 and counting

Subscribers: 298

Comments:

Amazing_Abby_xxx: GET BETTER, LUCYLOCKET xx ♥♥ xx

queen_dakota: Most pathetic video yet, loser! You could at least have brushed your hair!

ShyGirl1: We'll keep watching, don't worry! Amazing news about *Grease* xxx

animallover101: Go, Barbed Wire, go x

(scroll down to see 19 more comments)

Chapter Eight

Lucy lay in bed, staring at her Taylor Swift posters and feeling bored. Yesterday, after two days of feeling awful, her dad had taken her to the doctor who diagnosed her with a chest infection. As a result, she was off school and had been told to rest her voice.

'No blogging allowed—'

'VLOGGING, DAD!' she'd interrupted hoarsely. 'Blogging wouldn't be a problem!'

Since then, she'd slept loads, watched some YouTube videos (RedVelvet doing her boyfriend's make-up – that had definitely cheered her up for a blissful fifteen minutes) and daydreamed about Sam. She picked up her phone from her bedside table and groaned. Another message from Dakota. Maybe if she squinted her eyes it would look like a cute message from Sam – as if! Lucy had no idea who'd given Dakota her number, but the girl been sending her vile texts all morning.

9:05

> **Dakota:** Cnt believe u missed first *Grease* rehearsal!! Srsly lame! R u even ill???

10:25

> **Dakota:** Couldn't hack the pressure??
> Why don't you drop out or better yet drop DEAD!

Jeez, thought Lucy, coughing into her hand. *Would a 'get well soon' have killed her?*

10:35

> **Lucy:** Get lost!

Lucy texted back now.

Lucy: I'll be back at school soon!

She switched off her phone so that she wouldn't have to read Dakota's poisonous reply.

'Hi, Lucyloo!' said Maggie in a stage whisper, poking her head round the door. 'Are you dying? Daddy said I had to be quiet. Is it because you're dying?'

Lucy croaked a laugh – thank god for little sisters!

'I'm not dying, Mags – just resting. You want to come up here and talk to me?' She patted the bedcovers and her sister jumped up, sitting on Lucy's feet and emptying her favourite 'handbag' – a yellow plastic bucket containing some crayons and a *Frozen* colouring book – all over the duvet.

As she proceeded to talk Lucy through the various pictures – 'Here is Olaf, the snowman, and Elsa – and this is Elsa again, in a different outfit, and this is Princess Elsa

AND Princess Anna . . . ' – Lucy found herself drifting off into a cosy fug of sleep, Maggie's little voice chirruping along softly in the background.

'Is she awake?'

'Of course not, dummy – she's hashtag sleeping.'

'Her right eyelid is flickering.'

'We should let her rest.'

'As if – she'll want to talk to us! Hi, Lucy!'

Lucy opened her eyes and took in Abby's bright smile, Hermione's anxious look and Jessie taking a picture of her on her phone. She grunted and waved the phone away. 'Oh my god! W-what's going on?'

'Surprise! We've come to visit the patient!' said Abby with a grin, holding out a bunch of 'Get Well Soon' balloons.

'Permission to put this on Instagram?' asked Jessie, brandishing the photo of Lucy asleep. Her hair was stuck to her forehead at random angles and one side of her face was imprinted with a pillow mark.

'Permission DENIED!' croaked Lucy, taking the balloons and tying them to the chair by her bed. 'I I-look half dead! W-why aren't you guys at school?'

'School's over – it's gone five o'clock,' said Hermione. 'Tell us if you want us to leave, though.'

'N-no – it's great to see you guys! I've been SOOO bored. Maggie showing me her *Frozen* c-c-colouring book has literally been the highlight of my day. Oh, and D-Dakota sending me evil text messages, of course. I don't even know how she got my number.'

Jessie looked uncomfortable. 'Oh my god – sorry about that. She asked me for it at registration – said she wanted to contact you about doing a vlog collab together.'

'As IF she would want to do a collaboration with Lucy!' said Abby. 'I can't believe you fell for that, Jessie.'

'It did seem kind of odd,' said Jessie, frowning. 'What did the messages say?'

Lucy sighed, patting the bed so that Foghorn would jump up on to the duvet. 'The last one was gently and supportively (not) encouraging me to drop out of

G-Grease because I missed one rehearsal.'

The others rolled their eyes, and Jessie looked even guiltier. 'I am SUCH an idiot. I can help you change your number if you want?'

'Don't worry – I can handle Dakota. The thing is, I *am* tempted to d-drop out, so she's kinda right. I didn't particularly want to be in *Grease* in the f-first place, and I already f-feel so nervous about the whole thing.'

Lucy regretted the words as soon as they were out of her mouth. And she regretted them even more when she caught sight of Abby's face. She knew how badly Abby had wanted a part and here she was, complaining like a spoilt brat.

'I m-mean, obviously I'm r-really thrilled to be chosen,' stammered Lucy. 'It's just – I'm scared of p-performing in public, and Dakota's made it clear she's going to do everything in her power to make it r-really hard for me.'

'Lucy, don't be ridiculous. You were worried about vlogging, and see how well that turned out,' said Abby firmly. 'Anyway, if you didn't *really* want a part in the show, you shouldn't have auditioned.'

There was an awkward silence. 'Well, you're in now and I think you'll be great,' said Hermione quietly. 'And Abby's right – look how many YouTube fans you have already.'

'Although . . . reality check,' butted in Jessie. 'If Lucy doesn't post a new vlog soon, her fans might stop watching. They need regular content!'

'It's true,' said Abby, less sulky now. 'People keep asking me when your next vlog is coming. Even my brother and his mate were asking while they were filming their latest video. This week's prank was so dumb by the way – they literally covered my parents' room in newspaper and waited for them to walk in. Pathetic!'

Lucy smiled tiredly and sighed. 'Guys, I want to make a video, but I'm not allowed to – d-doctor's orders for the next week.'

'Man – that sucks!' said Jessie, pulling out a strand of gum and wrapping it around her finger.

'But . . .' Lucy continued. 'I w-was thinking, why doesn't

one of you step in for me, record a vlog we could upload on my channel. M-maybe you, Abby?'

Abby jumped up and hugged Lucy, her energy and excitement flooding back. '*Ohmygosh*, thank you, are you sure? It's such a good idea cos once RedVelvet was off with toothache and you know her friend CinnamonBuns? Well she did a vlog for her and even though it wasn't as good it kept the subscribers entertained—' She was interrupted by the laughter around her. 'What?' she asked innocently.

Lucy recovered first. It felt good to laugh, but not good for her throat! 'We're just excited b- by your enthusiasm, Abs, aren't we, girls?' She paused, then decided this was a good time to share her worries with her friends. 'I'm s-so relieved you're up for it – and there's another reason I want to keep up my views. Springdale City Farm, where my mom works, is at r-risk of closure. They've decided to put on a Halloween f-fundraiser event and I was thinking of publicizing it on my channel, so that people will hear about it and t-turn up on the day.'

'I can definitely do a mention about that,' said Abby, tapping a note into her phone. 'I'll get Prankingstein to talk about it too. Ooh . . . and maybe we can tweet a link of the vlog to RedVelvet and CinnamonBuns – they'll probably never see it, but we can try at least!'

'Wow, talk about reaching for the stars, Abs!' Hermione patted Lucy's bedcovers. 'Your poor mum must be worried sick, Lucy.'

Lucy nodded sadly. 'It's really rubbish. I'm s-seriously hoping we can do something to help!'

'Well, we'd better make sure the next few vlogs are AMAZING and draw in loads of new viewers, then!' said Jessie cheerfully. 'No pressure, Abby! What are you going to vlog about?'

'Well . . . I always thought I'd like to do a shopping haul, and I am actually going shopping tomorrow as I need SO MUCH STUFF right now . . . so the timing would be perfect!' said Abby gleefully.

VLOG 7

Abby's Shopping Haul
While Lucy's Off Sick!

12:45

FADE IN: ABBY'S BEDROOM – NIGHT

ABBY's room is large with lots of white and lavender furniture. Fairy lights and candles set the mood. She is sitting cross-legged on her double bed, surrounded by bags of shopping, wearing charcoal jeans and a black top, her blonde hair freshly blow-dried. On her lap is a tiny cream pug.

ABBY

Hi, everyone! You might have seen me before in Lucy's other vlogs. For anyone who doesn't know me, my name is Abby – nice to meet you! I'm stepping in for Lucy today because she's still ill and she wanted me to entertain you guys. At first I wasn't sure what to vlog about, but then I realized I could just show you my new gear! I LOVE it when RedVelvet does her amaaaazing shopping-haul vlogs, so hopefully you guys will like mine too (and I won't lose Lucy all her subscribers!).

Oooh! I also want you to meet Weenie, my darling pug. He's soo cute.

ABBY gives him a big kiss and he licks her nose.

ABBY (CONTINUED)

I love carrying him around in a handbag or basket. I just wish I could bring him to school with me, but not I'm not sure Mr McClafferty would hashtag approve of that!

ABBY laughs and grabs the bags.

ABBY (CONTINUED)

OK, so when I went to the shops this morning I was looking for two specific things as well as anything fabulous that might catch my eye. I wanted a new going-out top to wear with jeans, and a nail polish in a bright fun colour.

So . . . here's how I got on . . .

ABBY empties out all the carrier bags on to her lap.

ABBY (CONTINUED)

As you can see – the trip was a success! I saw this top in the

first shop I walked into . . .

ABBY holds up a butterfly-print T-shirt with capped sleeves and a zipped
pocket.

ABBY (CONTINUED)

Isn't it so pretty? I love the exposed zip too, which gives it a little

edge. It would look great with jeans and some hoops. What

else have we got here?

ABBY looks around
and grabs a short
kilt-like skirt.

So this . . . was NOT on my list of things, obviously, but I absolutely had to have it. Don't you love these pleats? I'm planning to wear it with thick woolly tights and biker boots.

There is a loud knock at ABBY's door and two fifteen-year-old boys come crashing into the bedroom and jump on to the bed. WEENIE starts barking.

ABBY

(CONTINUED)

OMG, Josh!
What are you guys
doing? You can't just
barge in—

JOSH

Hiyaaaa! Nice haul, Abby! Been spending all your savings?

ABBY talks apologetically to the viewers, but is giggling.

ABBY

Guys, this is my brother Josh and his friend Charlie – better known for their dumb channel Prankingstein!

JOSH

Are you doing a vlog, little sis? About time!

CHARLIE

Awesome! You need our help to shake things up a little?

CHARLIE grabs a jar of sweets off her bedside table and rattles it. ABBY laughs, despite herself.

ABBY

Noooo! It was going perfectly!

ABBY throws a cushion at CHARLIE, who comes and gives her a massive squashy hug until she squeals for mercy.

JOSH

I see you have some new lipglosses that need testing
immediately.

JOSH grabs a tube from her dressing table, opens it, brandishes it at
the camera and starts applying it to CHARLIE's lips. ABBY tries to snatch
it from him.

ABBY

No! That one's expensive! Stop it, Josh!

CHARLIE

But isn't it a great colour on me?

CHARLIE grabs the tube and starts applying the bright red to his eyebrows too.

ABBY

Guys! Get out! You're going to knock over the candles! Lucy will never let me do a vlog again!

JOSH

No worries, darling sis, we're out of here. Just one last thing . . .

JOSH grabs a bright pink new bra – part of ABBY's haul.

JOSH (CONTINUED)

I always wanted to try one of these.

JOSH holds it up against his T-shirt.

JOSH (CONTINUED)

Oops, need a bigger cup size – this one's tiny!

ABBY snatches it away and blushes bright red.

ABBY

GO! NOW!

JOSH

We're gone! Just thought we'd give you a hand.

JOSH talks straight to the camera.

JOSH (CONTINUED)

Look out for the new Prankingstein vlog – online

tomorrow – when me and Charlie surprise some shoppers

at the supermarket checkout . . . MWAHAHAHAAA!

JOSH jumps on CHARLIE's back and they piggyback their way out of the room with massive over-the-top waves to camera. WEENIE comes back out from under the bed where he's been hiding. ABBY clears up the bedspread, still blushing and breathless.

ABBY

Er, really, really sorry about that! What can I say – they are SOOO annoying. Anyway – what was I on about? Nail polish!

ABBY holds up three bottles.

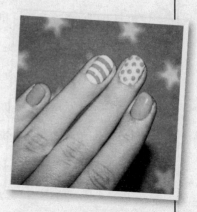

ABBY (CONTINUED)

I was only planning to get one, but there was a three-for-two offer on, and how could I resist these colours? Aren't they cool? This metallic one is called Silver Gleam, this light blue one is Blue Sky Dreaming and my favourite is this bright yellow – Sunflower Surprise! Even though it's September now, I thought it would be nice to keep wearing a summery colour on my nails. Then I'll move on to the other two later in the year. Is that weird, to match your nail polish to the seasons? Let me know in the comments down below!

ABBY picks up three stripy red boxes.

ABBY (CONTINUED)
My last purchase was these cute pick-'n'-mix sweets in this old-fashioned packaging – these are a present for Lucy to say get well soon, and thank you for letting me do my own vlog on your channel.

Oh, and by the way – I promised Lucy I'd mention this amazing Halloween fundraiser happening the Saturday before Halloween at Springdale City Farm. We want loads of you to come and enjoy the spooky fun – and cute animals – and raise tons of cash. So be there or be square as they say! Details down below.

Now I need to go and try on my new stuff . . . again . . . apart from maybe that bra . . . hashtag cringe! Say bye-bye, Weenie!

ABBY waves WEENIE's paw.

ABBY (CONTINUED)

Bye, everyone, have a great evening!

FADE OUT.

Views: 769 and counting

Subscribers: 425

Comments:

queen_dakota: Bet Josh looks better in that bra than you do. Fried-egg alert!

pink_sprinkles: I ❤❤❤❤❤❤❤ shopping! xx

HashtagHermione: Weenie, you rock.

animallover101: Weenie is so funny and cute! Is he named after the pug in the Eloise books?

Amazing_Abby_xxx: YES! He's amazing. Xxx

PrankingsteinJosh: Who are those incredibly fit boys?

PrankingsteinCharlie: I don't know but I want to see more of them!!

Amazing_Abby_xxx: Ha ha – you two are SUCH LOSERS!!

(scroll down to see 32 more comments)

Chapter Nine

'Are you sure you're ready to go back, pumpkin?' shouted Lucy's dad over the noise of her hairdryer.

She switched it off. 'D-Dad, I'm fine now – and it's the second *Grease* rehearsal this morning,' said Lucy. 'I can't miss it! And I have GOT to get out of this room before I turn into Barbed Wire and start hibernating.'

'Barbed Wire won't start hibernating until November, your mom says.'

'Whatever, Dad! I need to get out of here is my point!'

Lucy brushed and straightened her hair, before rushing down to feed Foghorn and grab some breakfast. She was dying to get into school – she'd show Dakota and the others that she meant business! Last night she'd watched *Grease* again and practised some of Frenchy's lines. She was such a fun, reckless character – the scene where she flunked out of beauty school and accidentally turned her hair pink was hilarious.

The Pink Ladies met Ms Kusama before registration.

'Thanks for coming in early, girls,' she said, slurping from a gigantic cup of coffee. 'I've got a busy day today, but I wanted to have a Pink Ladies catch-up now that Lucy's back. No Kayleigh, though? Has anyone heard from her?'

Dakota looked at Ameeka who shrugged.

'N-nope,' said Lucy.

The teacher looked exasperated. 'That's the second time she's been late. Well, let's make a start. Last time we looked at Rizzo's solo and today now that Lucy's here we can have a bash at the sleepover scene where they teach Sandy to smoke. I'll read Kayleigh's part for now.'

Kayleigh never showed up, but the rehearsal went well, with Ms Kusama throwing herself into the role and the girls following suit. Lucy's confidence soared and she cheerfully ignored the poisonous looks from Dakota when Ms Kusama praised her singing. It was amazing how much the vlogging had helped Lucy get used to speaking out loud – as soon as she accepted that her stammer was there it started to go away of its own accord. She had to admit that Dakota was really good too – as the snappy and impatient Rizzo she couldn't have been better cast – but at least she was way less annoying in character.

'How was it?' Hermione asked later during registration. Lucy could tell that Abby was listening too, and she tried not to brag about how well it had gone.

'It was OK! I'm s-still pretty terrified of learning my lines, though – you g-guys will have to help me. And Dakota looked like she was about to vomit when Ms Kusama told me I had g-great energy.'

'That's awesome,' said Abby. 'Sounds like you're doing really well – I'll definitely help you with your lines. And Dakota can go jump off a cliff.'

'Thanks, Abs,' said Lucy, touched. 'It would be so much more fun if you were in rehearsals too, though!' *Oops – wrong thing to say*, she realized, too late, as Abby's face fell.

'No need to go on about it. I didn't get in – who cares?' Abby snapped.

'Sorry, forget I s-spoke, OK?' Lucy snapped back.

Whoa, she hadn't expected Abby to be so touchy. She'd been about to compliment Abby on her haul vlog, but now maybe she wouldn't bother.

'Great vlog last night, Abby,' said a girl named Justine, strolling over to her desk as the bell rang.

'Oh – um, thanks!' said Abby.

'I love haul videos. It's so cool seeing what other people buy! I shared the link on Facebook last night and loads of my friends from my old school have subscribed.'

'Wow – hear that, Luce?' said Abby, lighting up. 'I took care of your channel like I promised – even got you some new fans!' Her voice had taken on a slightly taunting edge, but Lucy decided to rise above it and give her friend some praise after all.

'I watched – and you were amazing! A complete n-natural – and Prankingstein were a r-real laugh too, in their own special way!'

'That bit with the bra was hilarious,' commented another girl. 'The three of you were so funny together!'

'I know, I couldn't stop laughing at Charlie with that lipgloss!' giggled Justine. 'Abby, your face was priceless!'

As Abby laughed along with them, a tiny bit of Lucy suddenly felt insecure about the brilliant feedback Abby was getting – which she knew was ridiculous. Abby had helped her out, and done a great job of it, that was all.

'I'm never touching that lipgloss again . . . Those boys are SO annoying!' Abby said with a large grin. She had recently admitted to Lucy that she had a teensy crush on Charlie, but she had sworn her to absolute secrecy – knowing her brother would never let her hear the end of it if he found out.

As they left the classroom, Jessie linked arms with Lucy. 'So, my friend, what are we doing for the next vlog?'

'I actually just thought of s-something,' said Lucy. 'It's embarrassing, but I'm r-really happy to be back at school, not for lessons obviously, but be-because I was SO bored at home, and anyway I w-was thinking, why don't we do a "day in the life of a Year Nine" kinda thing? I've got my vlogging camera so we can record on that and just sh-share fun nuggets from our school day.'

'What, like double maths?' said Hermione sarcastically.

'Er, no, probably not that,' laughed Lucy, shoving her friend. 'More like – what we have for l-lunch, who's got the dodgiest posters in their l-lockers. Natural-look makeovers in the loo at b-break-time. What do you guys think?'

'Let's do it!' said Abby. 'Maybe check with Miss Piercy later to see if we're allowed to upload school footage, though. You have to be careful with that stuff.'

In assembly, Lucy found herself sitting in between Dakota and Ameeka after they'd pushed past her friends.

'Just wanted to say, you were decent in rehearsal

this morning,' said Dakota sullenly as a sixth-former read through some notices on the stage. It took Lucy a minute to realize Dakota was addressing her and not her friend.

'Er, th-thanks!' she said, surprised.

'Yeah, I think we'll have a good group dynamic actually,' Dakota continued. She swept her hair over one shoulder and started smoothing it with her hand. 'Sorry about those text messages, by the way. I'm just really impatient when people don't commit to stuff. But you've obviously been practising and you totally rocked it today.'

'Th-thanks!' said Lucy again, unable to believe her ears. Maybe Dakota wasn't that bad, deep down. She was still slightly suspicious, but decided to give her the benefit of the doubt. 'I'm really looking forward—'

'I also think your vlogs are getting better,' Dakota bulldozed on. 'I like the sound of that day-in-the-life thing you were just talking about with Abby.'

Aha! Maybe this explained the niceness – Dakota

wanted a starring role in the vlog.

'If I were you, I would actually film this assembly,' Dakota continued. 'Mr McClafferty is meant to be announcing something big apparently. I heard Miss Piercy talking about it.'

Lucy hesitated. 'Yeah . . . but d-don't you think Mr McClafferty might see?'

'Oh, you don't have to hide it from him,' said Dakota. 'He's actually really pro-social media . . . He loves it when students put photos and little videos on Instagram and sometimes he even comments on them. Great publicity for the school! Besides he loves the sound of his own voice so why wouldn't he want it recorded?' She laughed and tossed her hair.

Lucy couldn't argue with that last bit – the balding Scottish headmaster was very fond of rambling at length in assemblies, on everything from his thought for the day to favourite snippets of poetry and rules and regulations.

'Well, I'm up for it,' she said, and grinned. 'We could

actually m-make a pretty cool r-remix of assembly with my new editing s-software.' She'd convinced her dad to buy the software at the weekend as a treat for getting into *Grease*, and she was dying to try it out.

Dakota shrugged. 'Yeah, that could work.'

As Mr McClafferty took to the stage and began to make his announcement, Lucy switched on her vlogging camera, flipped up the flipscreen and started filming.

'W-welcome to assembly!' she whispered into the microphone.

'Hold it up higher,' urged Dakota, nudging her elbow. 'So you can see properly over everyone's heads.'

'Right!' Lucy held the camera up just as Mr McClafferty's announcement gathered momentum.

'And so,' he continued, projecting his voice self-importantly, 'it brings me great pleasure to announce – to announce – WHAT THE BLEEDING HELL?' He broke off and stepped towards the front of the stage and stared out into the crowd of students. A few tense moments passed as everyone tried to figure out what was going on. 'Are you . . . are you FILMING me, girl?' he bellowed.

Too late, Lucy gulped and lowered her camera. 'Y-yes, sir,' she stuttered as the entire school turned and gawped at her. 'S-sorry, sir?'

'This outrageous behaviour shall NOT be tolerated. Come up here and bring the blasted camera with you,' he roared.

Lucy thought she would die of embarrassment. She was also very confused. Her cheeks flaming, she got up and started to walk towards the stage. She received sympathetic looks from her friends in the row ahead, but she distinctly heard a soft sniggering from Dakota and Ameeka. Lucy's blood boiled.

'Oh, ha-ha, v-very funny,' she hissed at them. 'You are such slime!' She didn't know who she was more angry at – Dakota, for being such a vicious cow, or herself, for being so amazingly gullible! It was a long walk up to the stage and had Lucy not been so furious she might have been more scared. Mr McClafferty took the camera with a sarcastic 'thank you' and told her to see him in the office afterwards. She slunk off the stage and out of assembly.

Lucy was still kicking herself later in the head's office as she stared at the objects on Mr McClafferty's desk, Miss Piercy at her side. As well as her beloved vlogging camera, there were her phone and earphones.

'I w-was p-planning to ask for p-permission b-before uploading anything to the internet,' she insisted.

But the headmaster was having none of it. He seemed too outraged to utter a single syllable. As his eyes threatened to pop out of his head, Miss Piercy stepped in.

'Lucy had a difficult start to the term and it's been a pleasure to see her confidence grow. Of course she was ill-advised to film in assembly, and it is right that she is reprimanded for that, but I do think her hobby has many benefits.' Lucy sneaked her a grateful look. She'd spoken to her a few times about her vlogging when they were discussing her anxieties about public speaking, and Miss Piercy had shown a genuine interest.

'Thank you for your comments, Miss Piercy,' said Mr McClafferty in a chilling tone. 'However, I must insist that this girl's parents are notified and her equipment confiscated.'

'F-for h-how long?' piped up Lucy, avoiding eye contact.

'For as long as I see fit,' he snapped, sweeping the camera, phone and earphones into a drawer. 'That is all! We will see that your parents are informed.'

At lunchtime, Lucy sat miserably at the table. She had clocked Dakota when she'd entered the room, but she couldn't think of anything scathing enough to say . . . and she worried that she might stammer if she tried. Abby rushed to join her.

'OMG – are you OK? What happened after assembly?'

She acts concerned, but she loves the drama, thought Lucy with a flash of annoyance.

'I had my phone and c-camera confiscated – and my

parents have been advised to take away my laptop,' she replied, staring at her plate of chilli. 'They're g-going to hit the roof when I get home.'

'Too bad your hashtag fans will have to wait a little longer for your next vlog!' called Dakota from the next table. 'Hashtag WhereHasLucyGone! Hashtag I'mBored! Hashtag Let's All Unsubscribe And Watch A Proper YouTuber!'

Abby exploded. 'What a cow! It's literally pathetic how jealous she is. Ignore her!'

'She's right, though,' said Lucy. 'First I couldn't vlog because of being ill, and now it's going to be ages until I get my stuff back.'

'Don't worry!' said Abby, her eyes lighting up as an idea formed. 'I can do another vlog for you!'

'That's OK,' mumbled Lucy.

'No honestly, I don't mind. Maybe not another shopping one, but I could try out some beauty products? Ooh, or act out my favourite emojis – RedVelvet did that and it was so funny! I'm sure it would get you some new subscribers.'

Lucy was quiet. She felt like everything that mattered was slipping away from her. 'Back off, Abby,' she snapped suddenly, the words out of her mouth before she could stop them. 'Why don't you set up your own ch-channel, as you're so full of ideas? All your millions of fans could subscribe to that instead of mine.'

'What?' said Abby, surprised. 'Oh – no – I didn't mean . . . I was just trying to help.' She stared at Lucy, hurt written all over her face. 'I'm not trying to say that my vlogs are better than yours – or that I'm more popular.'

'W-whatever,' said Lucy with a deep sigh. 'It doesn't matter anyway.'

'Luce, come on!' begged Abby.

'Look, I'm just not in the best mood right now, OK?'

'Ooh-ooh! Trouble in paradise, losers?' said Kayleigh, overhearing.

'SHUT UP, KAYLEIGH,' shouted Lucy and Abby together. They exchanged awkward smiles, but before Lucy could find a way to apologize to her friend, Abby made an excuse, her cheeks flushed, and left the room.

Dear Morgan,

Look! I am writing you a letter. By hand. How old school is that?!

As you know from the message I sent from Hermione's phone I am CUT OFF from all internet life at the moment - it sucks!! Especially now that I am at home with nobody's phone to borrow!

I'm having such a hard time - I hadn't realized how much vlogging had become a part of my life, and now that I can't do it I'm MISERABLE. Vlogging is everything! Bet you can imagine how I'm feeling. I can't even watch your vlogs or anyone else's! Mom and Dad have confiscated my laptop. They think I've become obsessed and need some 'digital detox' time - whatever that is! All I know is . . . I'm miserable!

There was a weird situation with Abby at school today. She volunteered to do another guest vlog for me and I completely shut down the idea. We didn't have a major fight or anything – it was just a really awkward moment between us. Is it lame that I want to do the next vlog on my own channel? I know Abby's great, but it just feels like she's trying to steal the limelight and I'm scared of her taking over. This is really harsh of me to say I know – as she (and you) are the ones who got me into vlogging in the first place, and I owe her so much.

Guess I'm just furious about Dakota setting me up and not being able to vlog – and taking it out on Abby. I'll have to make it up to her!

Hermione is being amazing as usual – it was her idea to lend me her phone and let you know that I was still alive! Hope you're doing great and that this reaches you quickly via snail mail!! I miss you SOOOOO much. Let's Skype the second I'm allowed back online!!

Love,
Lucy xoxoxoxox

Chapter Ten

A few days later, Miss Piercy asked Lucy to stay back after English, the last lesson of the day.

'Here you are,' she told her, opening her desk and handing over Lucy's phone and camera. 'How did you cope without them?'

'It's been so hard! I actually had to write my f-friend in the US an old-fashioned letter!' said Lucy, resisting the urge to look at her phone immediately.

'Well, I'm sure that was good practice! Make sure you keep the camera at home in future – and phones are for break-time only.' Miss Piercy's voice softened. 'I have watched some of your vlogs, though, Lucy, and I think you're doing a great thing there. Keep it up!'

'Thank you, Miss P-Piercy!' It was a bit embarrassing to hear that her teacher had watched the channel – that *Frozen* vlog! – but at the same she time she felt a rush of pride. Lucy left the room walking on air, excitedly switching on her iPhone. It buzzed with messages and she saw a text ping up from an unknown number. The first line set her pulse racing and she clicked on it.

Wednesday 12:04

> **Unknown Number:** Hey, Lucy, Sam here. Bea gave me ur number. Heard u'd been ill. If you come 2 Springdale on Sat u want to go for hot choc after? Need to discuss fundraising ideas! Sam x

She jumped a mile. He'd texted her! He wanted to discuss fundraising ideas with HER. And the kiss at the end of the message – did that mean it was a kind of date? Then she panicked, realizing the message had been sent two days ago – he must think she was so rude not to answer. She started tapping out a reply.

'Got your phone back, then?' Hermione joined her in the corridor. 'Thought we could walk home together.'

Lucy kept tapping. 'Definitely. Just hold on a sec. Such a relief to have this b-back in my life, I n-nearly died without it!'

'Well, I'm glad you survived! That is the happiest you've looked in ages,' said Hermione, watching her closely. 'Who are you messaging anyway – Morgan?'

Lucy blushed. 'No.'

'Who, then? You seem pretty desperate to get in touch with them!'

'Er, just, you know . . . Well, it's n-not anyone you know actually—'

'Oh, wait – it's a boy right? Right? *Right?*'

Lucy laughed as she held the school door open for her friend and they stepped into the car park. 'OK, fine. Y-yes, it's a boy!'

'Yes!' Hermione said gleefully. 'Someone at school? Do the others know who it is?'

'No – and no!' said Lucy. 'There's n-nothing to tell!' She smiled at her friend who was staring at her closely. 'Anyway, your turn to s-spill!'

'Huh?'

'You must have a crush on SOMEONE – I see you d-daydreaming and staring out of the window in class ALL THE TIME.'

Hermione grinned, looking a little shy. 'Well, if we're talking ideal men, I'm going to have to go with Mr Darcy.' She ticked off his qualities on her fingers. 'Tall, dark, dashing, rich. He would build me an amazing library in his amazing stately home – and buy me signed first editions of every Harry Potter. If he could, you know, fast forward in time.'

Lucy laughed. Typical Hermione! 'Nice. And . . . w-what about in the real world? Jane Austen heroes aside?'

There was a pause. 'Nobody really,' shrugged Hermione, looking up and down the car park as if searching for Mr Perfect to magically appear from round the corner. 'To be honest I don't think I have anything in common with the boys here! They're sooo immature – I don't have time for that. Heathcliff from *Wuthering Heights*, though – now HE would be liven things up! Oh – and what about Viktor Krum from Harry Potter?'

'You're amazing,' giggled Lucy. 'Hey, I know! Why don't we do a f-friendship vlog this evening – ask each other embarrassing questions. Honest answers only!'

'What, just the two of us?'

Lucy paused. She should probably invite the others, but the Abby thing was still bothering her. 'Yeah, just us! I can't believe I d-didn't know about your weird literary cr-crushes until now – there has to be tons of other stuff we don't know about each other!'

Hermione looked torn – pleased to be asked, but slightly uneasy too. Lucy knew she wasn't the most comfortable of the four girls in front of the camera, but she actually came across really well in her cute adorable way.

'No *really* personal questions, I promise,' Lucy said. 'Just s-silly stuff. And we don't have to upload it if you're not totally happy with it – trust me, I have learnt my lesson about p-privacy!'

'OK, as long as I get to help choose the questions,' said Hermione. 'And I need to finish my book report first.'

'That's cool – come round later, whenever you're done. I'll start thinking of the questions – *mwah ha ha*! Er, only k-kidding!' she added seeing Hermione's alarmed face. 'I'll be nice!'

Back in her bedroom, Lucy was dying to finish her reply to Sam. But she was finding it hard to get the message just right and Foghorn, sitting on her lap, meowed anxiously when she read it aloud to him. In the end she messaged Morgan.

Lucy: It's meeee! Back on my phone 😊

Morgan: Yesss – about time! Got your letter – everything OK with Abby?

Lucy: Yeah, that was a bad day, but so much to fill you in on since then. Guess who texted??

Morgan: Ummm, does it start with an S?

Lucy: YES IT DOES!! 😊

Lucy: He asked me to go for hot choc 2 discuss fundraising for Springdale.

Morgan: WOOEEE!!!

Lucy: Not sure if it's an actual date, but still exciting right?? Here's what I'm gonna reply – does it sound OK?

Lucy: Hey, Sam, sorry 4 slow reply, phone got confiscated. Soooo cool to hear from you and hot chocolate is my favourite! Can't wait to discuss ideas! See you Sat. Luce xx

Morgan: Nice but a bit long!! And does he call u Luce???

Lucy: Er no! Maybe I'll just put L.

Morgan: Gotta play it cool. Don't say your phone got confiscated . . . just let him wonder what you were up to 😄

Lucy: Ha ha, this is why I love you! Thanks! Gonna catch up on some of your vlogs now so I can see your little yankee face!

Morgan: The last one is pretty awesome, even if I do say so myself! How to pamper in style. Enjoy!

Lucy sent the message to Sam then settled down in front of her laptop (also newly returned) to watch Morgan's home-made face mask vlog. She giggled as her friend plastered her face in blueberry and oatmeal gloop and placed two cucumber slices over her eyes, putting her slipper-clad feet up and grinning into the camera before biting into a massive cream cake. She looked completely insane! No wonder her subscribers loved her.

As the video finished, Lucy looked back at her phone and realized there was no reply from Sam yet. *Get a life*, she told herself. It's only been three minutes. And he might not reply at all – now that she'd agreed to the date. Not ACTUALLY a date, though! A business chat! And she'd have to remember not to mention her 'superficial' hobby . . . and pray that her stammer didn't get too bad.

Putting him out of her mind she started making a list of questions for Hermione. Boys could wait!

VLOG 8

Hermione and Lucy
Friendship Quiz!

11:30

FADE IN: LUCY'S BEDROOM – NIGHT

HERMIONE and LUCY are sitting on LUCY's bed. They have a pile of little scraps of paper between them, which FOGHORN keeps swatting with his paw.

LUCY

Hello, everyone! I'm f-finally back! Today me and Hermione are doing a f-f-friendship quiz for you guys. We've found out a lot about each other since she b-became my 'Guardian Angel' on the first day of school, and this is the ultimate test of whether we were paying attention.

HERMIONE

(*nervously*)

I don't know if I'm ready.

LUCY

You'll be fine. It's not an exam you have to revise for!

HERMIONE

OK, let's do it!

LUCY

S-so, what happens is, we take turns picking up a question from this pile. We then have to guess what the other person's answer would be, and then find out if we were right!

Good luck, H!

HERMIONE

Thanks – good luck, Luce!

LUCY

I'll g-go first.

LUCY picks up a piece of paper.

LUCY (CONTINUED)

Ooh easy one! What is your favourite food? Well, obviously
Hermione here is a b-baking legend, so I'm going to go
with CAKE!

HERMIONE

I love it, but it's not my favourite! Spaghetti
Bolognese is.

LUCY

(*snapping her fingers*)

Oh man, I knew that. You have

it like three times a w-week! You literally ate it yesterday! So
annoying. OK, so what's my favourite food?

HERMIONE
(*confidently*)
Peanut butter and jam sandwiches. You're always weirdly
thrilled when they're in your packed lunch.

LUCY
Ha ha, correct! That's embarrassing, I didn't realize I w-w-went
on about them so much!

HERMIONE
Sorry to break it to you, but they're totally rank. OK – my turn!

HERMIONE picks up a scrap of paper.

HERMIONE (CONTINUED)
What is your most embarrassing moment? Oooh, I don't know.
Well, I'm guessing your first day at school and the *incident* with

Dakota's video was . . . shall we say . . . a hashtag 'challenging'
time in your life.

LUCY

Oh m-my God, my stammer in f-front of my new classmates,
and everyone thinking I'd wet m-myself, *and* Dakota putting
it online. Yep, that has to be it. Along with countless other
s-stammering moments, but that has to be the w-w-worst,
having it broadcast on the internet.

HERMIONE

Nobody cared anyway!

LUCY

Don't worry, I'm over it now, you know, apart from the
n-nightmares, the cold sweats, the flashbacks . . .

HERMIONE

(*looking shocked*)

Are you serious?

LUCY
NO! I'm kidding! OK. Now *your* most embarrassing

m-moment . . .

HERMIONE looks uncomfortable.

LUCY (CONTINUED)
Hmm, you're pretty s-sensible really. Oooh – what about your

Grease audition when you forgot how to s-sing? Or there was

that time you slipped on a chip and dropped your tray in

the canteen . . .

HERMIONE

Both of those things were pretty excruciating, but no . . . the

worst one was before I met you.

LUCY

What happened?

HERMIONE

So, after an all-you-can-eat Indian meal, I went to the cinema

with my family and was feeling queasy for ages. By the time I

realized I was actually going to puke, it was too late and I hurled

all over the person sitting in front of me. They were *so* angry.

LUCY

(hands over her mouth in horror but giggling too)

Oh n-no! How did I not know about this?

HERMIONE

(*rolling her eyes*)

Well, it's not the kind of thing you go around broadcasting. My dad paid the woman fifty pounds to get her clothes cleaned and my whole family legged it before the end of the film.

LUCY

(*still giggling*)

Which f-film was it?

HERMIONE

Finding Nemo. I still feel sick if it comes on TV.

LUCY

Ha! Well, I'm learning *a lot* about you today! OK, n-next question.

LUCY picks up a scrap of paper.

LUCY (CONTINUED)

What is your favourite animal? Easy. Owl.

HERMIONE

(*holding up her owl-print rucksack*)

You know it! Ooh, but what's yours? You're an animal freak . . .

you like them all!

LUCY

I do have a favourite, though.

HERMIONE

Is it hedgehogs now because of Barbed Wire? Or cats . . . I can't

imagine you without Foghorn? I'm going with cat.

LUCY

Afraid not . . . you'll never guess . . . I love all animals

but my f-favourite's actually a s-s-sloth. I've seen loads of documentaries and I love how lazy and snuffly they are. They've got the longest arms too, for h-hanging from trees – it would be so amazing to get a sloth hug!

HERMIONE

Random! But they are kind of cute, I guess. OK, next . . . What would you do if it was your last day on Earth? Oh god, that's really hard. I literally have no idea!

LUCY

I know it sounds really b-boring . . . but I would probably just hang out with my family! Have an amazing takeaway – a massive D-Domino's with loads of sides. It's not what my parents would choose, but this is *my* dream scenario!

HERMIONE

Nice! And how would I spend my final twenty-four hours on this planet?

LUCY

You . . . would t-track down J. K. Rowling's address, visit her, get all your books signed and talk to her for hours about how she'd changed your life. Then go to D-Daniel Radcliffe's house and hang out with him.

HERMIONE

Ha ha, I like your thinking! Not my original answer, but it's definitely my plan now if I'm ever given twenty-four hours to live!

LUCY

Ha! And the f-final question – would you rather have three h-hands attached to both wrists or three feet at the end of each leg? I reckon you would choose . . . feet?

HERMIONE

(looking a bit blank)

Wrong – definitely hands! Think how many books I could hold. I'm guessing you would say hands too?

LUCY

Wrong! I want the f-feet – six feet equals three pairs of shoes – cue an epic shopping trip for all that footwear!

HERMIONE

But think of all the vlogging you could do with six hands – all those different angles at once.

LUCY

Good point!

LUCY looks back at camera.

LUCY (CONTINUED)

Thanks for w-watching, guys, and if I am ever in that situation I

will choose six hands so that I can deliver better vlogs to YOU!

That's how much I love you! Be sure to g-give us a thumbs-up

if you enjoyed this video, and let us know in the c-comments if

you want to see more quizzes on this channel. Byeeee!

LUCY and HERMIONE wave.

FADE OUT.

Views: 340 and counting

Subscribers: 450

Comments:

StephSaysHi: Best vlog yet!!

queen_dakota: Puke puke puke

jazzyjessie: Cnt believe Finding Nemo story! OMG OMG that is awkward 😜

ShyGirl1: You should ask deeper questions. About love and stuff.

pink_sprinkles: I love quizzes! You should do one with Abby and Jessie too! #squadgoals

(scroll down to see 15 more comments)

Chapter Eleven

23:26

Sam: Cool.

Lucy stared at the message on her phone as her dad drove her to Springdale. Sam had finally replied late last night, when she'd been busy posting her friendship quiz, and she'd been a little surprised by how abrupt his message sounded. And now as they approached the farm she felt her heart speed up – this would be the first time she'd seen Sam since he'd suggested a drink. What if he'd changed his mind?

And as if that weren't enough to worry about she'd

got a message this morning from Abby that had made her feel sick to her stomach.

8:15

> **Abby:** Is there a reason you picked H over me for the friendship quiz? Do you want me off your channel for good?

The message had made Lucy feel terrible – she'd known deep down Abby wouldn't like being left out of the quiz, but it was gut-wrenchingly horrible to see how hurt she was. She'd have to talk to her later.

When they arrived at Springdale, Bea asked Lucy to oversee the families visiting Pets Corner.

'Keep an eye on the younger kids and make sure they don't feed the animals anything apart from the food we sell. Actually, not just the kids. Last week while you were off I caught a grown woman feeding a goat a multipack of Mars bars – I ask you!' The freckly redhead rolled her eyes.

It was a fun but hectic day – and Lucy was only able to glimpse Sam from afar, busy with his riding lessons. She began to wonder if he'd forgotten about their plans, but was distracted by a visitor to the farm who recognized her from her channel and whose girlfriend was a fan.

'She's friends with someone who goes to your school, which is how she got into your channel,' he said. 'It would mean the world to her if you mentioned her in one of your vlogs – she thinks you're amazing. No offence, I don't really watch them, but I recognize you as they are literally on all the time!'

'That's so cool!' said Lucy, a little self-consciously. It felt weird but also really exciting to be recognized. She wondered if his girlfriend were one of the people who left regular comments on her vlogs. ShyGirl1, maybe?

16:30

> **Lucy:** I've just been #spotted!

She texted the others.

16:31

> **Lucy:** Remind me to do a shout-out to a girl named Essie!

As she put her phone away she was startled to see Sam standing in front of her. She was about to tell him about being spotted too, before remembering that YouTube was a no-go zone.

'Oh, h-hi!' she said instead. He was even taller than she'd remembered – with that same cheeky look in his eyes.

'Ready to get out of here? I am so done for the day!' he said. Lucy nodded nervously. She was as ready as she'd ever be, though she was pretty sure her hair was a disaster.

'Have fun, guys!' shouted Bea as they left together, causing the other volunteers to have a good gawp too.

Thanks for that, Bea! thought Lucy, getting more and more anxious.

Sam walked her to a nearby cafe with shiny red surfaces and cool vintage records framed on the wall.

It kind of reminded her of the diner set some of the drama students at school were making for *Grease*. As they were shown to a cosy little booth, she gave herself a pep talk. *No YouTube or vlogging chat, remember! And just take your time – the words will com*e.

Maybe Sam was a touch nervous too, she realized suddenly. There was an awkward pause once they'd ordered their drinks, and he looked down at his hands as he spoke.

'So . . . thanks for coming out,' he said shyly. 'I just thought since you mentioned it last time that you could, well, help me out with this fundraiser thing.'

'S-sounds like it needs to make a *lot* of money,' said Lucy. 'No pressure!'

'I know, right!' said Sam, his eyes sparkling. 'I mean, there are other measures in place too, but we definitely need to bring in the bucks!'

His jokey tone relaxed her and she felt a million times better. She caught sight of her reflection in the mirror near the booth and noticed her hair actually looked pretty cute, a few crazy wisps escaping her shiny topknot. She could talk to hundreds of people on her vlog – and she could do this, whatever *this* was – she still couldn't tell if it was a fundraising meeting or a date. Better not to assume anything.

'L-let's get brainstorming, then,' she said, taking a notebook out of her bag. 'Item one—'

'Actually, I'm just heading to the gents – but you start with some ideas, then present them to me when I'm back!' replied Sam.

'Yes, L-Lord Sugar,' she said, doing her best impression of an *Apprentice* candidate.

He chuckled.

We're definitely flirting, she thought, trying not to smile too widely. *Be cool, Lucy!*

As Sam slid out of the booth, he knocked his open rucksack on to the floor without realizing. Lucy bent to retrieve it, and seeing that a small package had fallen out she picked that up too. A card inscribed with the name 'Anna' was attached to the package, which was about the size of a jewellery box. And around the name was drawn a big heart in purple felt tip. Lucy's actual heart sank.

She froze, the box in her hand, before coming to her senses, putting it back and replacing the rucksack on Sam's seat. Calm down, she told herself – maybe Anna was his mom? But how many people call their parents by their first names? Could she ask him about it? No! That would be so uncool. Her next thought was to text Morgan. She would one hundred per cent know what to do in this situation. But she was interrupted by Sam returning and the waitress delivering their hot chocolates, overflowing with frothy whipped cream and mini marshmallows.

'So what've you got for me, then?' asked Sam playfully. 'Designed a brand logo yet?'

'Erm, n-no,' said Lucy, stirring her hot chocolate and desperately trying not to think about Anna. Why couldn't she focus?

'Oh – OK, then!' he said, sounding surprised at her lack of banter. 'Only kidding, obviously. No pressure for us to come up with anything today – I just thought it might be fun to kick around some ideas. It's a Halloween event so we need to think all things ghoulish and gross.'

She paused. 'OK.' She tried to make herself say something – anything – but it was like her brain had turned to mush, and all she could do was stare lamely at the marshmallows floating around on the creamy foam.

'Er, so,' Sam went on uncertainly, 'I was thinking we could do bobbing for apples, and witchy face paint for the little kids, that kind of thing?'

'Y-yeah. S-sounds good,' she mumbled unhappily.

'And, er, like guess the weight of the skull, ha ha?'

'OK. Yep.'

He stared at her, baffled. 'Look, you don't seem that bothered, Lucy?' he said coldly. 'I thought you were up for this. But, whatever. I can find someone else to do this with if it's not your thing.'

'It is, it's j-just I've g-got a lot on,' she said quietly, trying not to well up. *Say something positive*, she urged herself – but, again, she froze. What a disaster! She pictured herself in a rollercoaster hurtling towards the ground.

'No worries. Well, I'm going to head off now – see you next week.' Sam slapped a fiver down on the table, slung his rucksack over his shoulder and was out of the door in seconds.

Probably off to see Anna, thought Lucy in despair. She turned and looked at herself in the mirror. Yikes! No wonder he'd wanted out of there – she was wearing the same miserable expression Maggie wore when Dad switched off *Frozen* and told her to go bed. Anna on the other hand was probably totally hot, one of those girls with a lovely inviting smile – a beautiful vision who radiated warmth and happiness . . . What an idiot she'd been, assuming this was a date!

Lucy: Operation hot choc: full blown disaster!

Morgan: OMG what happened?!

Lucy: 5 minutes in and he's already left 😞

Lucy:

Morgan: Why??

Lucy: I think he's got a girlf. I was a mess.

Morgan: I doubt it!

Lucy: Forgot how to speak 😵

Morgan: Sorry, sweetie. Bet it wasn't as bad as u think tho.

Lucy: Trust me. EPIC FAIL.

After Lucy had finished messaging with Morgan, she allowed herself to wallow in her misery and replay the Sam disaster one last time. As she thought about the things he'd suggested for the fundraiser, a little spark of an idea went off in her head. OK, so the not-a-date hadn't gone so well, but she could still do something to help with the fundraiser. In fact, this was her area of expertise! She and the girls could do a Halloween-themed vlog – the perfect thing to get their viewers in the mood. Sam would disapprove, obviously, if he knew about it – but he didn't! And even if he did – who cared! She texted the girls and soon messages and Instagram pictures started flying in from Hermione and Jessie. Abby took a while to respond, but eventually she also chipped in, sending a picture of a 'Bloody Mary' make-up look they could try. Lucy immediately sent her a private reply.

15:15

> **Lucy:** Looks great! And sorry 4 being an enormous douchebag about the friendship quiz. Can't wait to do this vlog 2gether. Not same without you. Lxxx

There was a slight pause, and then a reply:

Abby: Me too! I love Halloween!

Still a bit frosty, with no 'x', but Lucy was relieved to see that Abby wasn't bearing a huge grudge over the quiz. She couldn't wait to see her bubbly friend and make things up to her in person.

VLOG 9

FADE IN: LUCY'S KITCHEN TABLE – NIGHT

All four girls are gathered around a flickering jack-o'-lantern on LUCY's kitchen table, wearing black, with more candles in the background. ABBY's face is painted a ghoulish white.

LUCY

Welcome to a freakkkkky vlog post in which we all get ready for H-halloween. We're doing it a couple of weeks early to give you guys some time to recreate our ideas. We're going to be talking costumes, make-up, tricks *and* treats! Abby is going to k-kick things off with a make-up tutorial for a 'Bloody Mary' look.

ABBY

Thanks, Luce! OK, this is quite a scary look, but it's actually simple to do. I've already covered my face with white face paint using a brush. Even my eyebrows are covered. I put my hair back with a hair band to keep it out of the way. Now I'm going to add a *lot* of black eyeliner along the top of my eyelids . . .

The girls watch and giggle, encouraging her to put more and more on.

ABBY (CONTINUED)

Finally, I have some fake blood to complete the look. I'm going to put a bit under my eyes, like this . . . and then a few drops here dripping down from my mouth, like a vampire that's just feasted. Done! What do you think, girls?

She turns and flashes them an evil grin. FOGHORN jumps up on the table, looks at ABBY, meows in alarm and jumps off again. Everyone laughs.

LUCY

N-n-nice! Well, not nice, but that's the point. Foghorn's clearly impressed. Next up we have Hermione who has p-prepared some yummy treats . . .

LUCY points the camera at HERMIONE, who is wearing an apron and has all her ingredients neatly set out in front of her. Everything is very organized.

HERMIONE

So I have some really easy but spooky-looking Halloween party treats to make. First of all, some disgusting Oreo Eyeball cookies. You just need a packet of Oreo cookies, which you take apart carefully. On each half that is covered with white icing you take some blue gel icing and make a circle in the centre. Pop a Smartie or M&M into the centre of the blue for the pupil. Then take some red icing and with a toothpick draw some little bloodshot veins on the white icing.

HERMIONE demonstrates this step by step.

HERMIONE (CONTINUED)

Don't they look rank? But they taste yummy.

MAGGIE walks in, picks one up, then walks out again. The girls all laugh.

HERMIONE (CONTINUED)

You're welcome, Mags! Hope you enjoy! Next up, Witches' Hat cookies. You need a packet of round chocolate-covered cookies – any kind you can get your hands on. You make some orange icing by adding orange food colouring into some plain vanilla icing.

HERMIONE makes icing and adds food colouring, then spreads it neatly on cookies.

HERMIONE (CONTINUED)

Make a circle of orange icing the size of a coin in the centre of the cookie – you can do this with an icing bag or with a spoon. Last but not least, put a Hershey's Kiss on the circle for the top of the hat. Bewitching!

HERMIONE giggles a bit self-consciously.

HERMIONE (CONTINUED)

Finally, a great idea for some spooky Halloween punch. Pour a bottle of Sprite into a punch bowl or any deep bowl. Add green food colouring. Then put in some scoops of sorbet and throw  in a handful of Nerds. The final gruesome touch is to add some eyeball sweets, which will swim around in the ghastly green mixture.

HERMIONE demonstrates this step by step too.

HERMIONE (CONTINUED)
Delicious!

HERMIONE steps back so we see all the treats set out nicely on the table.

HERMIONE (CONTINUED)
Be sure to give a thumbs-up to your favourite treat and send me pictures of your own versions on Instagram or Twitter.

LUCY
Wow, Hermione, you are amazing! I would n-never be able to make anything that looks so good. OK, next Jessie is going to show us an amazing trick. She hasn't told me what it is yet . . . Sh-she told me to come through into the other room so, Abby, can you bring the camera?

LUCY walks through the door and an enormous plastic jug of green slime, which has been balancing between the top of the door frame and the door, falls on her head. We hear LUCY shriek and the others squeal with laughter.

LUCY (CONTINUED)

EEEW! That was d-d disgusting.

LUCY wipes the slime out of her face and hair.

LUCY (CONTINUED)

I can't believe you just did that. Jessie!

JESSIE

(*spluttering with laughter*)

Trick or treat!

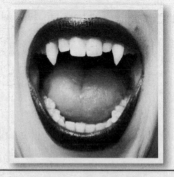

LUCY

(*still wiping away slime*)

If you say so! It's a good thing it missed the camera. Urgh! So before I go and have a much-needed shower, Abby has a fun s-surprise to end today's film. It's Weenie!

CUT TO: WEENIE in a bumblebee costume.

LUCY (CONTINUED)

Weenie is trying out his adorable Halloween costume. How cute is this? Wouldn't you give him a treat?

WEENIE yaps happily.

LUCY (CONTINUED)

Happy Halloween,
Weenie!
So, everyone, let us
know if you enjoyed
today's vlog. Be sure to give us a thumbs-up and let us know

what you l-liked best in the comments section below! And most importantly – I know I've mentioned this b-before, but we are helping out with a Halloween fundraiser at Springdale City Farm, where Barbed Wire came from, two weeks on Saturday. We'll all be there, Weenie too, with g-games, treats, pony rides – it's going to be amazing! So come along, bring your friends and we'll see you down there. Oh, and before I forget, here's a m-massive shout-out to our friend Essie! Bye-ee!

FADE OUT.

Views: 560 and counting

Subscribers: 478

Comments:

ShyGirl1: Thanks for my shout-out ha ha!! Hope I can make it to the fundraiser – I'd love to meet you.

lucylocket: ESSIE!! Knew that was you! Hi ☺

MagicMorgan: That was amazing guys!!! Happy Halloween!!

StephSaysHi: Weenie is adorable. Where did you get that outfit? I want one for my dog.

billythekid: Wish I could get SLIMED!

lucylocket: Be my guest!

lucylocket: OMG nearly 500 subscribers! 😄 😄 😄

queen_dakota: Slime = massive improvement on your regular look!

pink_sprinkles: Abby's vampire make-up was amaaazing. I'm awful with eyeliner 😵

Amazing_Abby_xxx: Just takes a bit of practice – u'll get there! Xxx

(scroll down to see 17 more comments)

Chapter Twelve

Next Saturday, Lucy and her dad picked up Hermione on the way to Springdale. She had offered to run the bake sale at the fundraiser and was attending today's planning meeting at the city farm. It had been a busy week with school, *Grease* and most of all their amazing Halloween vlog – which had taken loads of planning – and Lucy had almost forgotten the disastrous not-a-date with Sam. But now that she was back at Springdale she was starting to feel flustered. And she knew she had to tell Hermione about Sam.

'It's so n-nice of you to help out, H,' Lucy said as they walked towards the farm kitchen where the meeting was taking place. She was amused to see that her nerdy friend had brought along not one but three notebooks and an array of pens.

'So listen, n-no big deal, but just so you know, that guy I liked . . . '

'Aha! I wondered what had happened to him,' Hermione said, turning to look at Lucy, tripping and nearly falling in the mud. 'Wait – does he work here?'

'Well, yes, he helps out like us . . . and you'll probably meet him today.'

Hermione's face lit up. 'This is so exciting! More exciting than – than – the time Harry's name came out of the Goblet of Fire!'

Lucy laughed. 'I'm n-n-not sure if anything is that exciting – to you at least, H! Besides, I'm ninety-nine per cent sure he has a girlfriend named Anna. And w-we had a c-catastrophically awkward time last week, so I am officially p-playing it cool.'

'Interesting,' said Hermione. 'Only ninety-nine per cent sure?'

'You know what I mean! I'm almost positive. So don't say anything em-embarrassing, OK?'

'Lips. Sealed,' said Hermione, doing a zipping motion across her mouth, the delighted gleam still in her eye. 'I can't wait for our meeting, though!'

During the meeting, Lucy sat as far away from Sam as possible and ignored Hermione repeatedly mouthing 'IS IT HIM?' at her across the table. Afterwards, Bea told the girls to go and round up the llamas. As Lucy left the kitchen, she noticed a message flashing up on Sam's phone, which had been left on the counter near the kettle.

11:02

Anna: Luv u loads sammy xxx

Lucy flinched and speed-walked out of the room, desperate for some fresh air. It was so upsetting – her fantasies shattered for good – but at least she knew for sure now. *Sammy?* She consoled herself with the thought that she would never use such an embarrassing nickname.

'Lucy! Wait for me,' called Hermione, hurrying behind her.

Much to Lucy's dismay, Sam joined them minutes later to help with the llamas.

'I am so relieved you're here!' said Hermione anxiously. 'This one keeps spitting at us!'

Sam chuckled. 'It's all a matter of patience. They're tricky little blighters.' As he began herding the stubborn animals, Lucy kept her distance, unlike Hermione who chatted to him continuously, gesturing excitedly to the different animals. At one point Lucy caught Sam giving her a questioning glance, and she pretended not to see it. After the not-a-date from hell, what was the point of striking up any kind of friendship? She usually enjoyed her time at the farm, but today she just wanted to go home.

'Well, you're completely wrong,' announced Hermione

cheerfully once the llamas were penned up and Sam had gone back to the stables.

'Wrong? About what?' said Lucy.

'About Sam. I can see why you like him, by the way. He's *such* a gentleman.'

'I *don't* like him any more, and I'm n-n-not wrong!' Lucy replied angrily. 'He has a girlfriend! Let's go and w-wash our hands – Bea asked us to prepare the lunches next.'

But Hermione was persistent as they walked through the farm.

'He asked me if you were OK, and kept looking over at you while he was talking to me. You were being kind of rude, the poor guy.'

'H-he's not a p-poor guy and if he really wants to know how I am he can ask me!' snapped Lucy. 'Besides, I heard him say he hated YouTube so if he knew about my vlogging he'd like me even less. It's h-hopeless.'

Hermione shrugged. 'OK, I'm just saying . . . and I really think you're wrong about the whole girlfriend thing. Have you even met her?'

Lucy stopped walking, her cheeks flushed with anger. 'No, Hermione, I haven't *met* her, but I've seen a t-text from her on his phone, as well as a jewellery box in his bag with her name on it. With a f-freaking *heart* around it, OK? So I'm pretty sure I'm not wrong, and in all honesty I don't know when *you* became such an expert on boys. Real ones, I mean, not f-fictional characters in books. Have you ever even had a crush on a real person?'

Catching sight of the devastated look on Hermione's face, Lucy stopped talking abruptly. Where had *that* poisonous outburst come from?

'I'm s-sorry, H, I didn't mean it . . . '

'Don't worry about it,' said Hermione quietly, walking ahead of Lucy and staring miserably out at the llamas.

Lucy touched her shoulder. 'H, please – I should have shut up. I've been in s-such a bad mood since I saw that s-stupid text message this morning and it c-confirmed what I thought. Sorry I took it out on you! Are you OK?'

Hermione nodded, but didn't turn round, and Lucy could tell that her meanness had really hurt. She hated herself for doing that to Hermione, who had been such a loyal and supportive friend since her first day at school.

'Hermione, please,' she said, her voice cracking. 'I feel t-terrible . . . You are such an amazing person and I've treated you like crap! I'm just g-gutted about the Sam thing and worried about Mom's job . . . If the fundraising projects don't work and the farm shuts down, we might h-have to m-move again.'

Hermione glanced back at her, the hurt and anger slipping from her face. 'Is it that bad?'

'Yeah. I mean, I don't know . . . My parents won't g-give me a straight answer. I'm s-so worried, though. I hate not knowing if we're s-settled for good.' A tear trickled down her cheek and, noticing, Hermione put her arms round her. Lucy sobbed into her friend's shoulder. She vaguely noticed Sam looking over at them from the stables, but she was long past caring what he thought.

'I know,' said Hermione as Lucy wiped her eyes with a tissue, 'let's do something fun to take our minds off all this. For myself, I would prescribe a new fantasy novel with thousands of characters to get swept up in . . . but as this is you . . . I'm going to say – vlog, vlog, vlog!'

'Sounds good – I'm up for it!' Lucy's phone beeped. 'Wow!' she exclaimed, reading the message. 'You w-won't believe this! It looks like we've got something to celebrate . . . Abby's got a part in *Grease* after all. Kayleigh's been kicked out and Ms K has just asked Abby to take her place. Awesome! Abby's invited us all round to hers later – I'll bring my camera.'

VLOG 10

Pizza and Pyjama Party!

12:05

FADE IN: ABBY'S LIVING ROOM – NIGHT

All four girls are in onesies – ABBY's is a pug, LUCY's a black cat, HERMIONE's an owl, JESSIE a dinosaur. They are all squeezed on to the sofa. 'Hi!' they shriek, waving wildly.

ABBY

Welcome, welcome, fans of Lucy's channel!

Do you like our onesies?

HERMIONE

I can't believe you made me wear this.

Even I don't like owls this much.

LUCY

It's cute! And they had a special deal on so I c-couldn't resist.

(*looking to the camera*)

T-today we are celebrating cos Abby's got a

part in *Grease* – wahoo!

They all cheer loudly.

ABBY

So Kayleigh got kicked out for smoking in the break at

rehearsal. Apparently she said she thought it was hashtag

in character as a Pink Lady. Doh!

JESSIE

You'll be awesome, Abby.

JESSIE does a cartwheel.

JESSIE

Woohoo – is that the
doorbell? I think pizza
might have arrived.

HERMIONE

Jessie's got some pizza challenge thing she's forcing us to do . . .

why do you want to mess with perfectly good pizza, Jess?

JESSIE (CONTINUED)

Well, it's just a few extra toppings . . . I'm sure it will enhance

the taste sensation!

(*laughs wickedly*)

We've had a few people suggesting it, so it's only fair to our

viewers! Give the people what they want!

JOSH and CHARLIE arrive, each bearing boxes of pizza and sitting down
on the girls' laps.

JOSH

Girls, did you think about actually opening the door to the poor delivery guy, instead of just talking about the pizza?

ABBY

(*seizing a box from Charlie*)

Give me that! And get out of our vlog!

CHARLIE

Whatever you say, little pug! Fetch!

CHARLIE starts whistling and the pair chase each other around the room. Once ABBY has caught up with him, CHARLIE pulls the tail of her onesie.

ABBY

(*laughing*)

Get off!

LUCY

(*rolling her eyes at the camera*)

Those two!

JOSH

(*starting to open the pizza boxes*)

Anyone for a slice?

JESSIE

Wait, wait, wait!

JESSIE grabs the pizzas, runs out of the room.

JOSH

That was greedy! Gobble, gobble, gobble!

JOSH makes silly faces.

HERMIONE

She's going to 'customize' them, apparently.

ABBY and CHARLIE come zooming across the screen, still chasing each other.

LUCY

(*to the camera*)

So this is getting a bit out of c-control! We didn't plan on having these guys here! It was just going to be a f-fun girly night, with makeovers, face packs . . . and pizza . . .

JOSH

BO-RING! And now we've made it INTERESTING!

The camera goes into handheld mode as he grabs it and goes around interviewing all the girls.

JOSH (CONTINUED)

Hermione, what is the worst thing you've done today?

HERMIONE

I'd have to say, putting on this owl onesie!

JOSH

Good answer. Twit twoo! Lucy, what is your biggest fear?

LUCY

Well . . . w-whatever Jessie is putting on our pizza at this precise moment!

JOSH runs into the kitchen where JESSIE is rushing around putting toppings on the pizzas. She catches him filming and grins.

JESSIE

Hi, Josh! Do you want the first taste? This one WAS cheese and tomato . . . but I've given it a little something extra!

We see JOSH's hand accepting the slice.

JOSH

(*from behind camera, his mouth full*)
Tasty, tasty – ARGH, Jessie, *what have you done to it?*
Help! Save me!

JESSIE

(*taking the camera and pointing it towards herself*)
Chilli powder, mustard – extra hot, mixed with Tabasco.
Just a little kick!

JESSIE films JOSH running to the sink and chugging a glass of water.

CHARLIE enters the kitchen, sees what's happening and laughs.

CHARLIE

He's rubbish with spicy things. Let a real man handle this –

Jessie, you got another slice for me?

JESSIE

(*still filming*)

Sure do! Help yourself. Abby, get in here!

CHARLIE puts an entire slice in his mouth, grins, does the thumbs-up . . . ABBY rushes in just as he has to spit the whole thing in the bin.

JESSIE

(*casually eating a slice herself*)

Pathetic!

JESSIE's eyes water a little, but she styles it out.

JESSIE (CONTINUED)

Same topping as the boys – delicious!

LUCY

(*walking in*)

Jessie, you're getting pizza on my camera screen! Noo!

CUT TO: LUCY in her bedroom in leggings and a big cosy jumper, FOGHORN kneading her lap.

LUCY (CONTINUED)

Hi, guys, I've just got back from Abby's after s-staying over last

night . . . Hope you enjoyed that little snapshot of our evening!

We thought it was p-probably safer to keep the camera away

from all the food and drink that was flying around in the end.

What else did we have on our pizzas? Well, marshmallows,

crisps, more chilli powder, s-spicy hot peppers – it nearly

made me cry – but we all did b-better than Josh and Charlie,

soooo satisfying. We had to eat a gallon of ice cream to

recover! Then we had a massive pillow fight with the b-boys –

it was brutal. Link to their Prankingstein channel down below if you want to see more of them . . . and let us know if you'd like us g-girls to guest on their channel too!

I'm just vlogging today to (a) to let you know we all survived Jessie's pizza challenge . . . though I am never trusting her with f-food again! Or with anything! And (b) to remind you about the Halloween fundraiser at Springdale City Farm, which is only a w-week away. We've been working really hard to prepare for it and it's so important to raise enough f-funds to keep the animals happy and safe in their home. So if you're local, or you're an animal-lover, or if you're just looking for some Halloween fun, come along to Springdale next Saturday – there will be s-so much going on! And share this link around . . . we really need LOADS of people to show up.

OK, s-sales pitch over . . . I need to go downstairs and feed Barbed Wire who is getting to be quite chunky. Let me know down below if you're planning on coming along on the day. Are you coming, Foghorn?

FOGHORN

Meow.

FADE OUT.

Views: 798 and counting

Subscribers: 623

Comments:

billythekid: Charlie totally fancies Abby

Amazing_Abby_xxx: AS IF 😊

StalkerGurl: I fancy Josh! Come to my house for pizza any time . . . I'll put NICE toppings on 😄

queen_dakota: Hashtag lamest one yet

animallover101: I'm posting this around to spread word for fundraiser xx

lucylocket: OMG thanks, everyone! We've had so many views and shares!! ♥

(scroll down to see 34 more comments)

Chapter Thirteen

'Mom, where shall I put the stuff for the henna-tattoo stall?' shouted Lucy. 'Mags – get away from that donkey – he could k-kick you!' She put down her bags and raced over to scoop up her little sister, who was taking a dangerous interest in one of the Springdale donkeys' back legs. Her dad was coming later, and she couldn't wait until he arrived to help with Maggie – right now her mum was preoccupied with some raffle tickets and not listening to her. 'Mom! The henna stuff?'

'Don't worry, I'll take it over to the main area later,' said Sam, who was just arriving carrying a crate of Granny Smiths for the apple bobbing. 'Hi, by the way. Is this your sister?' He smiled at Maggie as he put down the box.

For some reason the anger and awkwardness Lucy had been feeling towards Sam vanished – maybe because she was in such a good mood today, and pumped up for the fundraiser. Girlfriend or no girlfriend, he was a decent guy, she had to admit – and seeing him in his Halloween-themed skeleton jumper made her giggle. Still so dreamy, even as a skeleton!

'Y-yep, this is Mags! Maggie. She's crazy about animals so we're going to have to watch her carefully today. Say hi to Sam, Maggie!'

But Maggie had already zoomed off squealing, 'I want to see the bunnies,' her little jack-o'-lantern wellies pitter-pattering in the mud.

'Ha ha, sorry about that,' said Lucy. 'I'm sure she wants to meet you – it's just—'

'Bunnies are cuter than me? I get it, don't worry. Heard it before and pretty sure I'll hear it again. I mean, they've got snuffly noses and a cute tail – can't compete with that!'

Lucy blushed . . . Was that a joke? Sam was the most chilled out she had seen him in ages.

'W-well good! As long as you're not feeling too rejected,' she replied with a smile. 'Oh, hey, Abs! Hey, guys!'

Abby, Charlie and Josh had arrived, carrying a massive GET YOUR SPOOKY MAKEOVER HERE sign, the boys draped in white ghost sheets and Abby with a full face of vampy Halloween make-up. 'This is my friend Sam, he's another volunteer here.'

'Hey!' said Josh. 'Pretty big day today, huh? Hope you don't mind if we do some vlogging while we're here?'

'Josh and Charlie have a YouTube channel,' explained Lucy hastily, hoping the conversation would end there. She had been planning to do some vlogging herself but secretly so Sam wouldn't notice. Though, now that she knew he was unavailable, maybe she didn't care so much what he thought about her hobby.

'So you wanna just film the day?' Sam asked the boys, looking a bit uncertain.

'Yes, mate, just us messing about and having a great time. We can send you a link if you want?' said Charlie. 'It might be good publicity for the farm.'

'They get quite a lot of views, don't ask me why,' said Abby teasingly. 'It's all a load of rubbish.'

'Shut it, Morticia!' said Charlie.

She grinned. 'Whatevs, Casper!'

'OK, well, no worries about the filming,' said Sam, picking up the crate. 'Do what you gotta do!'

'Cool,' said Josh. 'But first – breakfast!' He and Charlie ran off towards the hot-dog stand, their sheets flaring out behind them.

'I'd better go too,' said Sam. As he carried the apples away, Lucy mouthed, 'HE HAS A GIRLFRIEND,' before her friend could utter a single word.

'NOT SURPRISED – HE'S HOT!' Abby replied, forgetting to whisper the last bit. Overhearing, Sam turned round and grinned at Lucy.

'Abby!' groaned Lucy, looking down and pretending to read a text on her phone, her face on fire. 'Don't embarrass me! His amazing g-girlfriend will probably turn up later and I don't want to look pathetic.' It was the first time Lucy had voiced the thought out loud – would today be the day she'd have to endure seeing Sam snog the beautiful Anna? Luckily she was soon distracted by her mum coming over and panicking that nobody would turn up.

'No worries, Mrs L!' said Abby, her sunny smile looking decidedly odd on her deep purple lips. 'Like we told you, we've been plugging it on Lucy's YouTube channel and I even sent a link of the last vlog to RedVelvet.'

Lucy's mum chuckled. 'That's great, Abby. We've done some promotion on our website as well with local press . . . and it would be fantastic if some of your school friends turned up.'

Lucy hid a smile – her parents still didn't quite get the whole YouTube thing – and her mum rushed off after Maggie, who was now energetically scooping up some rabbit poo with her plastic spoon. Lucy thought her parents would be quite surprised if she knew how many subscribers and views the LucyLocket channel was getting these days.

Later, as the fundraiser was becoming busier, Lucy went to check on Hermione at the cake stand – the queue for the Halloween cupcakes was epic. She panned over the crowd with her camera and saw Abby and Charlie giggling as they tried to do a joint apple bob, both biting into the apple at the same time.

Very up close and personal, she thought, until Josh ruined the moment by filming them, and making loud kissing sounds. She laughed as Charlie ran after Josh, trying to snatch away the camera.

Next she went over to the pony-riding area, where Sam was organizing rides for some little kids. No sign of Anna yet, she noted, putting her camera down. She watched Sam carefully help a small boy off the pony who, overcome by the whole thing, burst into tears – but was quick to recover when Sam gave him a high-five.

Oh god, why does Sam have to be so cute? And so

perfect? Lucy's heart ached, until an unpleasant voice broke her out of her reverie.

'This mud is everywhere! EW! It's disgusting! Someone should clean it up!'

A familiar vanilla scent blended disagreeably with the smell of fried onions coming from the hot-dog stand.

'W-what are you doing here?' asked Lucy, turning round to see Dakota, Kayleigh and Ameeka teetering over towards her in four-inch heels and tiny skirts.

'Why shouldn't we be here?' snapped Dakota, accepting a tissue from Ameeka and trying to wipe the mud from her stiletto. When this didn't work, she handed the tissue to Kayleigh and pointed at the shoe, and to Lucy's amazement Kayleigh bent down and continued the job for her. Satisfied that her shoe was OK, Dakota looked up and noticed the pony riding. She flicked her hair in Lucy's face. 'You ask why we're here – well I couldn't help but notice the fit boys in your boring animal-saving video the other day. And if memory serves –' she looked at Ameeka, who stared at Sam then nodded – 'that was one of them.'

Lucy bristled. 'His name is Sam. But he has a girlfriend, so I w-wouldn't get your hopes up.'

'As if that's ever stopped Dakota before,' said Kayleigh with a smirk. 'Where is this girl anyway? We'll scare her off, no worries!'

'Don't get aggro, Kayleigh,' said Dakota cattishly. 'I've told you before it doesn't suit you. I can handle this myself. And you,' she sneered, turning to Lucy, 'don't delude yourself into thinking he'd ever fancy you!' And before Lucy could think of a reply, Dakota reapplied her lipgloss and sauntered off towards Sam, her catwalk stride slightly askew as she teetered on her heels.

Lucy glanced at Kayleigh in surprise, catching a hurt expression flash across her face before she stomped off in a strop. Lucy stared at Dakota's confident back. She knew that Dakota was full of herself, but this was taking things to another level. And even though Sam wasn't hers, and he had a girlfriend anyway, she felt a massive rush of annoyance and jealousy. Surely Sam wouldn't go for Dakota, she wasn't his type, but despite her absurd behaviour Dakota did look good . . . and there was no telling with boys.

'Hot-chocolate break!' announced Abby, as she and Jessie came over from their stand. Jessie, a gauzy veil over her head, had been telling people's fortunes after Abby had done their ghoulish make-up. Abby handed Lucy a plastic cup and then froze. 'OMG. Double OMG!'

'What is SHE doing here?' added Jessie. 'My crystal ball says . . . hashtag not invited!'

'She fancies Sam apparently. She saw him in my vlog,' said Lucy. 'She's literally just turned up in the hope of . . . I don't even know! And it's all my fault!' She almost felt like crying.

'He's not bad-looking, to be fair,' murmured Jessie.

Abby laughed. 'So we're all agreed that Sam is fit, then! I can't believe you never mentioned him to us before, Luce – even if he has a girlfriend. Although come to think of it I do now remember him from your vlog. I should have paid closer attention at the time,' she teased.

'There's nothing to tell – we've just h-helped out here together a few times. Hermione's met him,' replied Lucy defensively, her eyes fixed on the pair who were now chatting away. 'Anyway, I told Dakota about the g-girlfriend, but she wouldn't listen.' Lucy could see Dakota gesturing animatedly and laughing. It was unnerving how her usually hard cackle softened to a girlish giggle in front of Sam. And her hair was blowing perfectly in the breeze, glossier than it had ever looked before.

'Well, Sam doesn't seem to be missing his girlfriend right now,' observed Jessie. 'Maybe they split up?'

'Well, if they did, you need to get in there fast, Lucy,' squealed Abby. 'Not Dakota.' She caught Ameeka giving her a suspicious look. 'Can I help you? Mind your own business much?' When the girl turned away, Abby noticed something and lowered her voice. 'Oh my god, look at that pony – it's coming up behind Dakota!' A small but very stout pony seemed to have its sights set on the carrot in Sam's hand and was making a beeline towards him – with Dakota the only obstacle in its path. 'She hasn't noticed! Lucy, camera, now!'

When Lucy was slow to respond, Abby grabbed the camera and started filming. The pony was picking up quite a pace, and within seconds Dakota had been knocked flying amidst high-pitched squeals, and landed flat on her back in the muddy field. The people standing nearby burst out laughing and a look of rage darkened the pretty girl's face.

'*Ohhhh*,' breathed Jessie, who had thrown back her veil for a closer look. '*Thank you, thank you, little pony, for this unforgettable moment.*'

'And we've got it on camera!' shouted Abby, as Dakota flailed about on the ground, kicking out at Kayleigh who had rushed over to help her up. Sam was doing a fairly rubbish job of trying not to laugh. 'Just think, Lucy – this can be your revenge for Dakota's first day at school video. It's perfect!' She was actually clapping her hands with glee. 'I'm getting Hermione! I can't believe she's missing this. Jessie – keep filming. She's dropped her purse now! Oooh, she's *sooo* angry! Ahahahhahaha this is the best day in the world!'

By the time Abby returned with Hermione, Dakota had finally got up out of the mud, helped by a still-trying-not-to-grin Sam, and walked off, her entire left side coated in mud and her perfect hair in ratty little tails. Kayleigh tried to put her arm round her, but she shook it off angrily, accepting assistance from Ameeka instead.

'I can't believe you didn't warn me, Kayleigh,' she was growling.

As they all limped off, Kayleigh could be heard trying to defend herself.

'Sorry you missed it, H! Highlight of the year,' said Jessie. 'It was so good I was cry-laughing. But don't worry – we have it on film. Watch this space!'

'So, Hermione, what was it you were trying to tell me?' asked Abby.

'Well,' said Hermione, who Lucy noticed was looking rather excited. 'I've seen something . . . someone . . .

important. I think so, anyway. I was really busy with the slime-green muffins, they were selling so well, and then I looked up at my next customer and, basically, well, er, I think RedVelvet is here?'

'*What?*' shrieked the other girls after a stunned pause.

'*You think?*' added Jessie.

Hermione shrugged. 'Well, I'm telling you, I was really busy so I can't be positive, plus I haven't watched as much of her stuff as you guys have, but . . . well . . . I'm pretty sure it was her. And you know how she always wears red? Well, she had on this red shirt . . .'

Abby flapped her hands in front of her face. 'Oh my god, guys – I tweeted her the links to our vlogs about today. Maybe she actually saw them.'

'Are you SURE, Hermione?' asked Lucy.

Hermione sighed. 'She definitely looked familiar. And quite a few people were pointing at her.'

The others stared at each other.

'W-well, w-what are we doing standing here?' said Lucy. 'To the bake tent!'

'Get the camera out! We have to capture this!' cried Abby. 'Arghh! I feel sick!'

But there was no RedVelvet to be seen at the bake tent and they couldn't find her anywhere else. It became harder and harder to look as suddenly there seemed to be lots of people arriving. At one point Lucy caught a glimpse of her mum looking delighted as she emptied the cash box to make room for more entrance money. She went over to talk to her. 'It seems one of your YouTube girls has mentioned our day on Twitter,' said her mum. 'I don't know what reach this RedVelvet has, but a few families have mentioned that they're here to see her. Very strange, but we are grateful. Do tell her if you see her.'

'It's true! Apparently R-R-RedVelvet tweeted that she was here!' cried Lucy, rushing back to her friends. 'That's why all these people are s-suddenly showing up.'

Abby immediately took her phone out to check. '*Just arrived at Springdale City Farm fundraiser – cutest animals!!* her Twitter says! And she uploaded a picture of a baby rabbit like two minutes ago! OMG, OMG!

Quick – we need to get to the petting zoo!'

The girls charged over, despite Lucy's mum calling to them to resume their duties on the various stalls. As they arrived at Pets Corner, they noticed a crowd of about five girls surrounding someone who was crouched down petting a baby lamb. 'It's her! It's d-d-d-definitely her!' said Lucy, her heart in her mouth as she caught a glimpse of a cherry-red shirt. They moved to the front and as she looked up, even more beautiful in real life, her dark eyes gleaming, they could only stare.

'Hey – you're the girls from the Halloween vlog, right?' said RedVelvet. 'The ones who tweeted me about today?'

'YES!' shouted Jessie. 'We LOVE YOU!'

'Th-thank you so much for coming,' said Lucy quietly, while Hermione remained speechless.

'I tweeted you! I didn't think you'd actually come!' cried Abby.

RedVelvet stood up, having finished handing out the bag of animal feed. Lucy gazed at her trademark red lipstick, so perfectly applied. She was stunning! Her fans often compared her Rihanna and Lucy could see why.

'I can't stay for long, I'm afraid,' she said, 'but I was in the area, and animals are really important to me—'

'I KNOW! WE LOVE BAMBI!' said Abby, referring to RedVelvet's bichon frise who often featured in her vlogs.

'Aw, thanks – he couldn't make it today unfortunately – and he's such a baby this lamb would probably freak him out,' she said. 'Anyway, I have to go and launch my new perfume in a bit. Wish I could stick around here instead, but I wanted to come and say hey and hopefully give you some publicity.'

'I think you've achieved that,' said Hermione, finally finding her voice and gesturing at the people around.

RedVelvet grinned. 'Awesome. Oh – and I also wanted to say you guys were really cute on the pyjama party vlog. How long have you been vlogging? Do you all have your own channels?'

'W-well, it's kind of my channel and I haven't been d-doing it very long,' said Lucy after a shocked pause (they couldn't believe RedVelvet had seen one of THEIR videos), 'but the girls do g-group videos with me a lot, like the one you saw.'

'That's so cool. Do you upload stuff regularly?' RedVelvet seemed genuinely interested.

Lucy grinned and looked nervously at the others. 'I try but I'm k-kinda new to this, and I s-sometimes find it h-hard to have time to make a n-new vlog. With school and everything.'

'Tell me about it,' said RedVelvet with a warm laugh, 'and I'm not even at school. I can't imagine that kind of pressure at your age. Well, why don't you guys set up a group channel, so that you can all share the responsibility of running it?'

'Sounds cool – how would that work?' asked Abby.

'Well, you can each take turns to vlog on different days, so there's no pressure on one person to keep it going. You can agree on weekly themes and continue doing your collab vlogs too. You'd have to find an awesome group name as well!'

Lucy smiled. 'Th-that would be amazing. If you guys wanna help out, I m-mean?'

'SOOO ready to do that,' said Abby, an earnest expression crossing her ghoulish face. Lucy winked at her.

'Hashtag, totally!' cried Jessie, flicking her veil.

Hermione looked unsure. 'I guess . . . so!' The others laughed.

'You'll be fab, H – you could have your own book-review slot,' said Lucy, and Hermione's face lit up. Just then RedVelvet's phone buzzed.

'I need to head off,' she said reluctantly. 'My driver is waiting out front and we need to get to London by five. See you guys later – and I'll make sure to subscribe once your channel is up and running. Maybe we can do a collaboration one day. Group hug!' She gave the girls a hug and left, stopping to take a few selfies with fans on her way to the exit.

'Oh my god,' said Abby, staring after her. 'Did that really just happen?'

'I think it actually did!' said Lucy. 'And I think I might be about to f-faint!'

'Don't do that – I don't have any smelling salts,' said Sam, walking over to the petting zoo with a girl who looked about eight and was dressed as a witch. 'What's going on? Apparently some YouTube person was here? Red something?'

'RedVelvet! She's really famous! We just chatted to her – it was INCREDIBLE, and she's going to help us set up our own channel,' babbled Abby. 'Well, it's Lucy's channel, really, that we're transforming into a group one.'

Sam looked at Lucy, confused. 'Lucy's channel? You're into this vlogging thing too? How come you never mentioned it?'

'Well, I heard you say once h-how superficial it all was so I didn't think you'd exactly b-be impressed,' said Lucy, not knowing where to look.

Jessie rolled her eyes at Sam. 'Well, get impressed, mate, because it's down to Lucy that RedVelvet came today. She vlogged all about it.'

'I'm VERY impressed,' said Sam softly, looking at Lucy. 'We both are, aren't we, Anna?'

The young girl nodded with a big smile. 'Can we see the goats?'

'Of course we can,' said Sam as the cogs in Lucy's mind started to turn. 'Girls, this is my sister, Anna. She's come for the Halloween Parade – isn't she the scariest witch you've ever seen?' As Anna hid shyly behind him, the girls cooed over how sweet she was. Lucy could tell that she had Down's Syndrome – as she had a cousin with the same condition.

'So . . . THIS is Anna,' she said softly. 'That g-gift . . . was for her?' Lucy felt as if she'd been struck by lightning for the second time in ten minutes. Could it be true? Had she been completely wrong about Sam having a girlfriend?

'What gift?' asked Sam.

'When we were in the cafe that time –' Lucy noticed Hermione dragging the other two away to give them some privacy – 'your bag fell on the floor and I saw a g-gift for Anna. I kinda thought it was for your g-girlfriend?'

Stop talking, she told herself. *You sound like a stalker!*

But Sam didn't seem to mind, though he did look quite surprised. 'Er – yeah – that was a bracelet for Anna's birthday. Show Lucy your special birthday bracelet, Anna.'

The little girl emerged from behind his back holding up her left wrist on which was dangling a charm bracelet, dripping with gold stars. A huge wave of relief swept over Lucy. She couldn't believe how happy she felt.

Thank you, thank you, she thought.

'It's because I call her my star,' said Sam. 'Kind of cringey, but there you go!'

Lucy smiled. 'It's beautiful. It really suits you, Anna, and you are the b-best witch I've ever seen!' Anna was so pleased that she demanded a hug from Lucy, before heading off to see the pygmy goats.

Sam cleared his throat, looking at Lucy questioningly.

'So wait. Is that why . . . you were acting so weird that day?'

Lucy blushed and looked over to where the girls were doing a pretty bad job of pretending not to stare at them. 'M-maybe. Sorry. I'm an idiot.'

'Hey,' said Sam. 'No, you're not. You've managed to draw in the crowds today with your amazing YouTube action – and you've just earned yourself a new fan over there,' he said, gesturing at Anna. 'And, as it happens,' he coughed, 'I've always been kind of a fan too.' He ran his hand along his T-shirt collar. 'Look, I know there's a lot going on today, but shall we try that hot chocolate again next week?'

'OK,' said Lucy with a big grin. No doubt about it, this time it was definitely a date. 'As long as you d-don't mind me vlogging the whole thing? JUST KIDDING!' she added as she saw the expression of terror on Sam's face. 'I'll leave my camera at home.'

VLOG 11

We Meet RedVelvet and Springdale is saved!

7:20

FADE IN: LUCY'S BEDROOM – NIGHT

LUCY, ABBY, JESSIE and HERMIONE are sitting on LUCY's bed talking to the camera. They all wave.

LUCY

H-h-hi guys. So we are here to introduce *the most exciting vlog ever*—

JESSIE

Hashtag EVER!

ABBY

Hashtag UNBELIEVABLE!

HERMIONE

Hashtag IT IS PRETTY GOOD.

LUCY

We've edited together some b-bits we filmed at the Springdale
fundraiser to show you how our day went. It was fantastic
and we met an exciting person who has been a m-massive
inspiration all along. It was unbelievable! (Morgan – if you're
watching – you will die when you see who it is.) But, before we
reveal all, we also have some Very Important News.

ABBY

Yes! We wanted to let you know that we are officially
launching . . . our own group channel! Ta-da! So me,

Luce, Hermione and Jessie will take turns to vlog on different days . . . and we'll also continue to do our group videos too. That way we'll be able to satisfy your demands for more vlogs and upload more regularly. We are *sooo* grateful for all the wonderful feedback we've been getting from you. So now . . . without further ado . . .

JESSIE and HERMIONE hold up a sign with GIRLS CAN VLOG painted in massive sparkly letters.

ABBY (CONTINUED)

Here's the channel name – we hope you like it. We think it's pretty kick-ass! The channel is up already, so get subscribing, guys!

LUCY

It's so exciting . . . and it's all d-down to that very inspirational person who gave us the idea, and the confidence to really go for it. We are going to make this channel a winner! So if you like the idea, p-please subscribe! And now . . . here is the montage of our amazing day – and THAT amazing person. ENJOY!

CUT TO: LUCY's handheld footage of the beginning of the day: Prankingstein bobbing for apples, having a mock fight with each other and JOSH pouring the water over CHARLIE's head . . . ABBY and CHARLIE biting into the same apple . . . people gorging on Halloween cupcakes . . . children in the fancy-dress parade . . . REDVELVET taking selfies with the girls and animals . . . ABBY pretending to faint . . . a sneaky shot of SAM and LUCY chatting . . . LUCY'S MUM shouting, 'It's been a huge success! RedVelvet made a very generous donation!' . . . LUCY, ABBY, HERMIONE and JESSIE doing a handstand, all in Halloween make-up and grinning at the camera and waving at the end.

FADE OUT.

Views: 11,059 and counting

Subscribers: 1,029

Comments:

MagicMorgan: OMG. You guys!! DYING OVER HERE.

lucylocket: Emailing you right now, M! Didn't want to spoil the surprise. X

***jazzyjessie*:** ONE THOUSAND SUBSCRIBERS, GUYS!!!!!

StephSaysHi: This didn't happen?!!! For real?!!

animallover101: WOW WOW I'm so happy for you guys! And Springdale is saved ☺ ♥

RedVelvet(verified): Yay, Girls Can Vlog! Loving your work already – xxx

pink_sprinkles: Arghhhh RedVelvet you are so gorgeous!

Amazing_Abby_xxx: Woohoo, Girls Can Vlog! Who's already subscribed?? ☺

(scroll down to see 195 more comments)

Morgan!!

So you saw the vid and now you get the full scoop!!!!

But first, sorry I've been so crap at keeping in touch in the last couple of weeks. It's been soooo craaazy – but good crazy. The *Grease* rehearsals on top of school and prepping for the Halloween fundraiser have been taking up all the hours of the day and then there's the vlogging!

I can hardly remember what it was like before I started – and I have you to thank for it all: the camera for starters and then the bullying (I mean the encouragement ☺). Without you I just wouldn't have had the nerve to film myself. And I've discovered I LOVE making videos and expressing myself as well as making new friends. Sometimes it's a bit scary, but it's always fun!

It's definitely helping me to control my stammer and *Grease* is going way better than I'd hoped. Dakota is still totally vile of course, and always trying to put me down if I mess up, but I'm handling it better.

In fact, I've decided not to take my sweet revenge on her — although I could. You won't believe it but she came to the fundraiser and was trying to chat up Sam in her short skirt and stilettos (on a farm — I ask you!) and she fell on her butt in the mud and looked a complete mess! *Sooo* funny and everyone saw. Abby even filmed it and wants me to post it on YouTube, but, to be honest, I actually felt a bit sorry for her, maybe because Sam was laughing at her too — so I won't be doing that — well, for the moment!

Anyway . . . I'm sure you're going to skip to this bit of my email anyway! REDVELVET!!!!!!!!!!!!!!!! I couldn't believe she'd really come. I still can't believe it. It was AMAZING and I literally forgot to breathe. Abby tweeted her and she saw our pyjama party vlog. She is *sooo* gorgeous in person but she's also so friendly and warm and normal. She was chatting to everyone and letting people take selfies and seemed really concerned about the farm and its animals – which is staying open as you'll have seen – WOOHOO!

We'll be launching GIRLS CAN VLOG properly really soon – it's crazy exciting and maybe one day you can be part of it too? RedVelvet also had lots of useful tips and pointers on vlogging, which will be really helpful. One day I hope she'll let me interview her on the channel. Wouldn't that be awesome? I would totally invite you if that happened.

So it was a perfect day, but I am saving the best for last . . . Have you guessed???? It's Sam! Or better yet Sam and Lucy or Lucy and Sam!!! He doesn't have a girlfriend – that was me jumping to conclusions. Again! Anna is his very adorable little sister and he is so sweet with her. And, more importantly, he LIKES me!! He really likes me! He's asked me out on a date and he's been texting me ALL THE TIME. I'm so excited, and a bit nervous too, to be honest – I hope I don't mess this up!

I am sooo happy, Morgan! I wish I could hug you to bits! It's late and I need to get to sleep. Skype tomorrow?

Love Luce, X ❤ X ❤

Top Ten Tips for Making Your Own YouTube Videos

Here are a few things to keep in mind if you're just getting started, like Lucy and the gang!

Please be aware that to set up a YouTube account you must be at least thirteen.

1) EQUIPMENT

All you need is a camera that can film in HD (high definition) and you are good to go! Most phones have such good cameras that many YouTubers just use their smartphones when they are starting out. More established YouTubers tend to use Canon cameras, however these can be expensive.

TOP TIP: If you are planning on investing in a camera especially for vlogging, make sure you do your product research *before* you spend any money. You can find loads of really useful camera and product reviews on YouTube.

TOP TIP: Don't forget the charger, a spare battery and an extra memory card.

Most computers come with editing software built in – with Windows Movie Maker on PCs and iMovie on Macs. These programs are great places to start! It's important to hone your editing skills and make sure your videos are as slick as possible!

TOP TIP: Careful editing is more important than having an expensive camera.

2) CHOOSE THE PERFECT USERNAME

Choose a name which connects to your Facebook/ Instagram/Tumblr/Twitter, etc., so your fans on other channels can find you. Your channel name can be changed as many times as you like, but your URL will stay the same, for example, Tanya Burr's URL is *Pixi2Woo*, but her channel name is Tanya Burr. See?

3) QUALITY OVER QUANTITY!

Upload a few well-made, well-thought-out videos. Take your time on them. Fight the temptation to make a hundred in a week!

4) BUT . . . BE CONSISTENT

If you have a new video out on the same day of the week, people will know to tune in on that day. One or two per week is great, or even one a month – you could do the last Friday of every month, for example.

5) LIGHTING, BACKGROUND AND MUSIC

The lighting can affect the quality of your video. I know! Who knew? It might be worth waiting for the perfect light to come through the window so your video will look the best it can be. Or if you have to vlog later in the day or in the evening, use lots of indoor lights, tea lights or fairy lights to get the right look.

WARNING: If you decide to use candles or tea lights,

make sure they are kept well away from any flammable materials and are placed on a heatproof surface. Never leave a burning candle unattended. If in doubt, blow it out.

Keep backgrounds light and uncluttered. White backgrounds are good.

Music is a trickier beast. When adding music to your video, you need to make sure you only use copyright-free music unless you ask for permission from the creator. Alternatively there is music available from the YouTube audio library which is copyright free, and lots of tracks you can find that use a Creative Commons license.

TOP TIP: Make sure you credit the musician in your description box.

6) THUMBNAILS ARE REALLY IMPORTANT

A cool, easy-to-read thumbnail will make more people click on your video. It should include your title and a screenshot from your video, or even a picture that you have taken especially for it.

TOP TIP: You can edit your thumbnails on specialist websites such as picmonkey.com.

7) TITLE YOUR VIDEO

Come up with a fun title for your video so that people can find it when they search for certain things, for example, 'smoky-eye make-up tutorial' or 'my favourite books'.

TOP TIP: Make sure you fill in your description box and as many relevant tags as you can. This is really important for discoverability.

For example, if you're doing a smoky-eye tutorial, you could mention in your description box what you are doing, what products you used and where you bought them. You could even provide links to websites if they are available online. Or if your video is about your favourite books, you could put in Goodreads links.

8) LENGTH

Eight to ten minutes is a good rule of thumb, but shorter

or longer is fine as long as you have plenty of interesting content . . . which leads us to . . .

9) CONTENT

Hopefully Lucy and her friends will have given you a few ideas . . . but the main thing to remember is to vlog about something YOU love – so do whatever floats YOUR boat. Stuck for inspiration? Here are some ideas:

Make a vlog about one of your favourite **ROUTINES**. Getting up, getting ready for bed, making breakfast, a tour of your room or even what's in your school bag!

QUESTION-AND-ANSWER SESSIONS with friends or family and **CHALLENGES** also make good subjects for fun videos, and there are plenty of **TAG VIDEOS** floating around YouTube which can be a great way to take part in the community.

Is there **SOMETHING YOU ARE GOOD AT**? 'How to' videos of gymnastics, baking, make-up or playing an instrument are great topics.

TOP TIP: Watch other YouTubers who inspire you. And don't pigeonhole yourself into being a specific type of vlogger, for example, someone who only makes videos about beauty or baking. Go for whatever YOU want to do and people can get to know the different sides of your personality.

10) GET INVOLVED!

It is a good idea, as a YouTuber, to get involved in the community as much as you can. Commenting on and subscribing to vloggers similar to you, who might also be just starting out, can be a great way to make online friends. This will also help you as they may check out your videos too.

AND ALWAYS REMEMBER . . . STAY SAFE ONLINE! Check with your friends and family that they are happy for videos they feature in to be shared online BEFORE posting. And NEVER give away your identity, address or details of your school – so don't wear your school uniform when vlogging.

Turn the page to read an extract from . . .

GIRLS CAN VLOG

Amazing Abby
Drama Queen

Coming soon!

'I hereby call the first official meeting of Girls Can Vlog . . . to order,' shouted Abby, leaping on the bed and banging her hairbrush against her bookcase.

'Whoa – easy there, hashtag chairperson!' giggled Jessie from where she lay stretched out on the carpet, a bowl of sour cream and onion pretzels precariously balanced on her stomach. 'That was loud!'

'Well, I had to stop you lot gassing away somehow!' said Abby, plumping herself back on to the bed with a grin. 'Anyway, now that I've got your attention – AHEM! – your ATTENTION . . .' She stopped talking and glared at Lucy and Hermione, who had discovered Abby's basket of nail polishes and were busy trying out different shades on each other.

'It's OK, Abby, we're l-listening!' said Lucy, as Hermione muttered something about pink not being her colour. 'What's the f-first item on the agenda?' Ever since they'd decided to switch Lucy's channel to a group channel, Abby had basically appointed herself team leader – and they were all happy to let their outgoing, bubbly friend take charge, especially Lucy, who was looking forward to a well-earned break from running a channel on her own. The way she'd battled with her stammer and her confidence issues by vlogging had been a source of inspiration to them all. Now they would all take turns, vlogging on different days, alone or in groups, to grow the Girls Can Vlog fanbase together.

Abby clapped her hands. 'First up is . . . our subscribers! How to give them videos they'll LOVE and how to get our numbers up!'

'Actually, I'm glad you've raised this,' said Hermione, blowing on her nail polish and using her other hand to nudge open the pages of a notebook. 'I've thrown together some statistics and, although we haven't uploaded any content yet, the Girls Can Vlog channel already has fifty-four subscribers. I cross-checked against Lucy's subscriber list and most of them come from her channel.'

'Yeah – a few p-people left comments saying they would f-follow us right away,' chipped in Lucy. 'N-not as many as I'd hoped though. Feels a bit d-depressing going from over a thousand subscribers to fifty-four.'

Jessie jumped to her feet, upturning the bowl and scattering pretzels everywhere – much to Weenie's delight. 'Let's not panic. The key, my friends, is content.' She gestured dramatically to the skies. 'Content, content, content. People only subscribe to a channel once they know what they're getting – and want . . . CRAVE to see more of it! So we need to send a clear message about Girls Can Vlog delivering five-star fun from our very first vlog.'

'Which we are recording in a minute . . . so let's get thinking,' said Abby. 'Jessie, you've got those Halloween sweets left over – food challenges are always fun – and we all need to come across as really chatty and friendly.' Her eyes rested on Hermione, who was still flicking through her notebook.

'What? So, OK, I'm not always that chatty,' Hermione sighed, looking up from under her fringe and catching Abby's eye. 'But sometimes I think it's best when we just act like ourselves. So what if I'm kind of shy sometimes?

Don't we want people to like us for who we are?'

'Hermione's right,' said Lucy. 'We can't all be mega-ch-chatty all the time. Anyway, I think the f-four of us balance each other out r-really well!'

Abby nodded and flashed an apologetic smile at Hermione. 'Totally. I just meant we should keep our energy up. We *are* great together!'

'Ooh – SPEAKING of being "great together" . . . anything you'd like to share with us, Luce?!' said Jessie.

'YES, LUCY,' said Abby meaningfully.

Lucy blushed. 'I have n-no idea what you mean.'

'You don't? Oh, my mistake – I was under the impression you'd been on this, like, super-hot date with the guy you'd liked, massively liked, for weeks, and it was pretty much the most exciting thing that had happened to you in ages, and yet you failed to update your besties within twenty-four hours—'

'Leave her alone, guys!' cried Hermione. She lowered her voice. 'Maybe the reason Luce hasn't told us about it is she didn't have the perfect time she was expecting?'